GIRL ELEVEN:

VANISHED

(A Maya Gray Mystery—Book 11)

Molly Black

Molly Black

Bestselling author Molly Black is author of the MAYA GRAY FBI suspense thriller series, comprising eleven books; of the RYLIE WOLF FBI suspense thriller series, comprising six books; of the TAYLOR SAGE FBI suspense thriller series, comprising eight books; of the KATIE WINTER FBI suspense thriller series, comprising eleven books (and counting); of the RUBY HUNTER FBI suspense thriller series, comprising five books (and counting); of the CAITLIN DARE FBI suspense thriller series, comprising six books (and counting); of the REESE LINK mystery series, comprising six books (and counting); of the CLAIRE KING FBI suspense thriller series, comprising seven books (and counting); of the PIPER WOODS mystery series, comprising five books (and counting); of the GRACE FORD mystery series, comprising seven books (and counting); of the CASEY BOLT mystery series, comprising five books (and counting); of the JADE SAVAGE mystery series, comprising five books (and counting); of the TESSA FLINT mystery series, comprising five books (and counting); of the CLARA PIKE FBI thriller series, comprising five books (and counting); and of the ELISE CLOSE psychological thriller series, comprising five books (and counting).

An avid reader and lifelong fan of the mystery and thriller genres, Molly loves to hear from you, so please feel free to visit www.mollyblackauthor.com to learn more and stay in touch.

ISBN: 978-1-0943-9797-9

BOOKS BY MOLLY BLACK

ELISE CLOSE MYSTERY SERIES
BEHIND HER LIES (Book #1)
BEHIND HER SMILE (Book #2)
BEHIND HER SECRETS (Book #3)
BEHIND HER GATES (Book #4)
BEHIND LOCKED DOORS (Book #5)

CASEY BOLT MYSTERY SERIES
BROKEN (Book #1)
FLAWED (Book #2)
BLEMISHED (Book #3)
DAMAGED (Book #4)
TWISTED (Book #5)

GRACE FORD MYSTERY SERIES
NEARLY MINE (Book #1)
NEARLY SAFE (Book #2)
NEARLY FREE (Book #3)
NEARLY GONE (Book #4)
NEARLY HIS (Book #5)

CLAIRE KING MYSTERY SERIES
ONCE HE SEES (Book #1)
ONCE HE LONGS (Book #2)
ONCE HE TAKES (Book #3)
ONCE HE FEELS (Book #4)
ONCE HE KNOWS (Book #5)

MAYA GRAY MYSTERY SERIES
GIRL ONE: MURDER (Book #1)
GIRL TWO: TAKEN (Book #2)
GIRL THREE: TRAPPED (Book #3)
GIRL FOUR: LURED (Book #4)

GIRL FIVE: BOUND (Book #5)
GIRL SIX: FORSAKEN (Book #6)
GIRL SEVEN: CRAVED (Book #7)
GIRL EIGHT: HUNTED (Book #8)
GIRL NINE: GONE (Book #9)
GIRL TEN: WANTED (Book #10)
GIRL ELEVEN: VANISHED (Book #11)

RYLIE WOLF FBI SUSPENSE THRILLER
FOUND YOU (Book #1)
CAUGHT YOU (Book #2)
SEE YOU (Book #3)
WANT YOU (Book #4)
TAKE YOU (Book #5)
DARE YOU (Book #6)

TAYLOR SAGE FBI SUSPENSE THRILLER
DON'T LOOK (Book #1)
DON'T BREATHE (Book #2)
DON'T RUN (Book #3)
DON'T FLINCH (Book #4)
DON'T REMEMBER (Book #5)
DON'T TELL (Book #6)

KATIE WINTER FBI SUSPENSE THRILLER
SAVE ME (Book #1)
REACH ME (Book #2)
HIDE ME (Book #3)
BELIEVE ME (Book #4)
HELP ME (Book #5)
FORGET ME (Book #6)
HOLD ME (Book #7)
PROTECT ME (Book #8)
REMEMBER ME (Book #9)
CATCH ME (Book #10)
WATCH ME (Book #11)

RUBY HUNTER FBI SUSPENSE THRILLER
IF I RUN (Book #1)
IF I TELL (Book #2)

IF I LIVE (Book #3)
IF I FORGET (Book #4)
IF I RETURN (Book #5)

CAITLIN DARE FBI SUSPENSE THRILLER
COME GET ME (Book #1)
COME FIND ME (Book #2)
COME TAKE ME (Book #3)
COME CATCH ME (Book #4)
COME SAVE ME (Book #5)

REESE LINK MYSTERY
BEYOND REASON (Book #1)
BEYOND REACH (Book #2)
BEYOND REPAIR (Book #3)
BEYOND DOUBT (Book #4)
BEYOND NORMAL (Book #5)

CHAPTER ONE

Laura Gibson hunched over the desk, looking at the DNA of a killer.

She was going through the DNA evidence carefully, wanting to make sure that she didn't miss anything. It was vital to be thorough, vital to make sure that everything was perfect, so she sat in her office, reading the results, making comparisons, making notes the old-fashioned way, with a pen in a notebook, rather than on the university's complicated online platform. She hunched over her desk, brushing a strand of long, brown hair out of her eyes, and kept working.

It was getting late, and outside, the moon shone, nowhere near full, though, not yet. It shone in a pearly white crescent against the dark backdrop of the night sky. Laura shuddered slightly at the associations that thoughts of the full moon brought into her head. She thought of the Moonlight Killer and all the havoc he'd wrought with the fifteen murders attributed to him. Fourteen now, supposedly, since the FBI agent who had caught him had managed to solve one that proved to be the work of another killer.

Fourteen was still more than enough to make Laura shiver as she stared at the evidence.

Laura shook her head. She wanted to just finish up and go home. The forensic science department at the university was empty at this time of the night, this whole corner of the campus largely dark and silent, away from the dorms and the frat houses, the bustling life of the rest of the place. She could have given up on her work right then, but it was important to finish checking her work before it went in front of the most critical audience of all in the morning: her students.

At 39, Laura had been a professor of forensic science for more than a decade now, long enough that she could probably have coasted through the work if she'd wanted to. She knew that plenty did, putting out the bare minimum of research, teaching only when they absolutely had to, putting out the occasional paper but not producing anything groundbreaking.

But it was also a world where reputation was everything. The last thing Laura wanted was for some student to stand up in the middle of her class and point out that she'd gotten something wrong.

Her nightmare scenario was one where she lost all authority for most of the rest of the year that way. Probably, at least a couple of students would swap classes, and once that started happening, the dean usually wanted an explanation. The last thing Laura wanted was to get her position put onto the long list of things that he might think about cutting the next time the university found itself short of funds.

Of course, she was catastrophizing. That wouldn't actually happen, but Laura was determined to make sure that it *couldn't.* Getting the details right was important. Laura sighed and went back to checking the sequences, wanting everything to be perfect. No, she'd gotten it right, there were no flaws here. Well, not except the one that she'd picked up on in her work as an occasional expert witness, showing that the police had made a mistake in the case. Laura felt a note of relief at that, because she always wanted her lectures to be as perfect as possible.

She could head home now, but what was waiting for her there? A cat, a research paper that she probably needed to finish in the next couple of days if she was going to get it into the next edition of one of the major forensics journals, a manuscript for a textbook that needed more editing before it went out to her publishers. Maybe a bottle of wine, but no one to share it with, and probably just leftover takeout to go with it.

Or she could head down to the lecture theater, get some of this up on the boards there, and save herself a quarter of an hour's work in the morning. The prospect of another quarter of an hour's sleep was tempting, especially if she was going to drink the wine. It wasn't as if the janitors would scrub away any of her work this late, the way they might have if she'd put it on there earlier. They could be very hit-and-miss about whether they obeyed the words "DO NOT ERASE" no matter how pointedly someone wrote them on the boards.

Laura rose from her desk, stretching out some of the tighter kinks in her muscles, her athletic frame complaining at being still in one spot for so long. She would cycle home, so she would at least get some exercise today, and maybe there would be a chance to fit in a proper run tomorrow.

There was something eerie about the university as Laura made her way over to the lecture theater, so that it was like making her way through the lifeless carcass of some great beast devoted to learning. Not that the lifeless necessarily felt odd to Laura, when she spent so much of her time working on forensics, refining and perfecting the techniques that might be used to catch the most dangerous criminals.

At least, that was the pitch she'd always given her family when they'd asked her if it was really worth it to go into academia like this, to move halfway across the country to teach a bunch of college kids the finer points of fingerprint and DNA analysis, the possibilities held out by analysis of insect life in crime scenes, the ways in which blood spatter analysis was pseudoscience best left to the TV and how important it was to be thorough about every detail of a crime scene, because you never knew which element might lead the police to a killer.

She made her way through the corridors, heading for the lecture theater. Occasionally, she saw lights on here and there in other buildings, pointing to other members of the university's staff working on their own projects until late in the evening, and there were plenty of lights around the library, where no doubt students were frantically trying to write papers at the last minute, but there wasn't anyone else in this part of the campus. Laura might as well have been alone on an alien planet.

Laura reached the lecture theater, clicking on the fluorescent lights closest to the front so that they bathed the lectern and the boards in a glow as sterile as one of the science labs. She didn't bother with the rest of the lights. No point in wasting energy when there was no one in there but her.

Banks of seats led down towards the front, where a lectern stood, a couple of microphones linked into the room's sound system. Laura checked that those were in a position to unclip easily, and that they had enough battery charge to walk well away from the lectern. She liked to pace the front of the hall as she talked, rather than being stuck in one spot with her notes. Probably, her students thought that it made her one of those professors who tried too hard to be interesting, but Laura didn't care.

Laura took those notes now and started to draw on the board, setting out some of the central points and key features to look out for. The actual DNA sequences, she would project, because that would allow her to slide one on top of the other, making the key difference between them obvious.

She wondered how many of her students would notice that difference before then, how many would guess that they were the same and then find to their shock that the two sequences were ever so slightly different. It was a crucial lesson in all forensic studies: that it was better to be precise and systematic than to hope that the human eye picked up everything. Too many wrongful convictions had happened because of that all too human tendency.

Laura put the pen down for a moment. She was pretty much finished now. She stepped back to look at her work, and that was when she heard a sound out in the darkness of the lecture theater. It sounded like someone moving there.

“Hello?” she called out. “Is there anyone there?”

There was no answer, while no further sounds of movement came from up there in the seats. Even so, Laura stared out at the dark lecture theater, her eyes straining as she hoped to catch some glimpse of whoever was there.

“If this is some kind of joke, it isn’t a funny one,” Laura said, in the stern tone she normally reserved for those students who were late handing in assignments. She hoped that it would lead to someone stepping out and announcing themselves instantly. It didn’t.

There was still no answer, still no sign that there was anyone there. Maybe Laura had imagined the sound. After all, wasn’t a part of the point of her lecture tomorrow that the human brain’s tendency to jump on patterns meant that it couldn’t be relied upon? That people tended to invest moments with meaning that wasn’t there? Maybe there had been a perfectly normal sound, creaking wood, or something caused by the building’s aging pipework, and Laura had added a bunch of fears and assumptions to those sounds.

Yes, she told herself, trying to fight down the spike of fear that had started to rise in her. That had to be it. It was her brain playing tricks on her, the shadows of the lecture theater conspiring to make her feel worries and fears that she otherwise wouldn’t. Everything was fine. She turned back towards the board.

Almost as soon as she did it, the lights near the front went out, plunging the whole lecture theater into darkness. Laura cried out, in spite of herself.

"This isn't funny!" she snapped, but she wasn't about to stay around and debate this with whoever had turned off the lights. She needed to get out of there now. She would find out who had done this later once she was sure she was safe.

The darkness wasn’t total. There was still a sliver of light coming in through the open door that led back to the corridors. Laura started to make for it, hurrying up the steps, not caring that she'd left her notes behind. She had her phone with her, so she used that for more light. As soon as she got out of there, she was going to call campus security, was going to find out who was doing this and…

Laura felt the moment when a wire went around her throat, felt the cruel edge of it bite into her flesh. She felt herself dragged back off balance, the violence of it wrenching her from her feet. She fought against the wire, feeling it cutting into her. She scrabbled at it, but she had no way to get behind it, had no leverage to fight against it.

She didn't even have enough time to call out for help before the blackness claimed her.

CHAPTER TWO

Maya waited with the stillness of a predator, watching the old warehouse through binoculars, looking for any signs of movement, willing this to be the place, for her hunt to finally be over.

She was currently crouched out of sight on the rooftop of a nearby building, wearing dark jeans and a hooded top, her FBI-issue bulletproof vest underneath it so that it wouldn't be immediately obvious that she was law enforcement if she had to head down to ground level. She kept herself in the shadows, her dark hair framing features that often struck people as too youthful looking for thirty-five years old. At five feet ten inches, she was tall for a woman, so she had to keep herself crouched low to make sure that she didn't draw any attention.

The last thing she wanted right then was for anyone to see her coming.

Maya had been up there for hours now, with the kind of patience she'd learned in military intelligence, back when she'd been watching possible insurgent positions or staking out locations for signs of high value targets. The same patience served her well as an FBI agent, but still, it was hard to push back the urgent need to simply charge in there and clear the warehouse with a gun in her hand. If Francis Hanratty was in there somewhere, Maya wanted to get inside and take him down.

She pushed aside that thought the way she had a dozen times now. She forced herself to be patient, to focus on the mission she'd set for herself. She scanned her surroundings, pausing every so often to make sure that she had good routes off the rooftop, and that no one was trying to approach her position. She had no doubt that if Hanratty spotted her up here, he would try to kill her.

That was what the Moonlight Killer did, after all. He struck silently, he killed quickly, and he was gone again before anyone could find him. It was daylight rather than a full moon, but Maya suspected that wouldn't make a difference if he thought she was an immediate threat. He would strike and kill her without warning.

After all, she was the one who'd sent him to prison, who'd been one knife-edged decision away from killing him in revenge for kidnapping her sister and twelve other women. Now that he'd escaped with the help of his followers, if he saw her, he wouldn't risk the chance that this time, she was playing their deadly game for keeps.

Maybe she would be. Maya kept telling herself that her goal was to put Hanratty back behind bars, but there was a part of her that kept insisting that the world would be a better place without him in it.

Maya looked down again and was surprised to see that there was finally movement there in the warehouse. The door had opened, and a single figure came out. Not Hanratty, but another man, tall and skinny, bald and wearing a long, dark trench-coat over jeans and a t-shirt. Maya recognized him as the warehouse owner, Philip Middlen. She'd seen his photograph in FBI files and had watched him go in there an hour before.

Her contacts said that he was a man who didn't care what he kept in the storage units within. Drugs, guns, people, it was all the same to him. Now that Maya knew more about Francis Hanratty, now that she'd started to pick apart his network, she knew that he'd used one of Middlen's spaces before. So why not again, now that he was on the run?

She needed to know for sure, though. She needed information about what she might face in there, and she needed it now. The time for waiting was at an end. She couldn't stake the warehouse out forever, which meant that she only had a couple of other choices.

Making a decision, Maya left her hiding place, making her way down from the roof along a disused and rusting fire escape that creaked with every step she took down it. She slipped along an alleyway, bringing Middlen back into view, a little way ahead of her. He was walking quickly now, as if he were on his way to an appointment somewhere and didn't want to risk being late.

Maya stayed behind him, trying not to get too close. It would have been easier to follow him with a full team, but it was just her out there, so she had to do her best to stay unobtrusive while still keeping Middlen in sight.

For a few hundred yards, Maya thought that she'd succeed, then Middlen ducked into another alley, suddenly breaking into a run. He'd spotted her, either realizing that something about her was wrong, or just reacting to the same person being behind him through the twists and turns of the streets.

She had an instant in which to decide whether to follow him or not. Protocol and safety both said that she should back off: if he'd made her, then Maya didn't know what kind of danger she was walking into by following him. He might try to attack her or lead her somewhere he had backup to try to deal with the problem of being followed. The other, more determined, part of Maya wasn't about to let go of this chance to find the Moonlight Killer, even if it meant throwing herself headlong into trouble. She would do whatever was necessary.

Maya broke into a run, following Middlen at speed, determined not to let him get away. She sprinted down an alley, weaving around trash cans, not caring now that he looked back and saw her following. Middlen took a left, then a right, glancing back over his shoulder as if hoping that he might have lost Maya. He knocked over another trash can as he passed so that it would be in Maya's path, but she hurdled it with ease, barely breaking stride. She might spend her days working cold cases and running other agents in an FBI field office, but she still had all the strength and athleticism that came from her background in the military.

Maya was closing on her target now, eating away the ground with every stride, her arms pumping, her hair streaming behind her. She could feel her heart beating rapidly, the exertion of the chase mixing with excitement and a hint of fear. She overrode the latter, following Middlen around another corner, determined not to slow down even for a moment.

As soon as Maya rounded the corner, she knew that she'd made a mistake.

He was there, waiting for her, turning and reaching into his jacket for a weapon. Maya could have gone for her own Glock, but then it would simply have been a contest of who could draw quicker, and even if she proved faster, she would be left with no choice but to fire. There wouldn't be any way to question Middlen then, and it would raise far too many problems with her superiors when they found out.

Instead, she powered forward, slamming into her quarry, smashing him back against the wall of the alley in a tackle before hooking his leg and sending them both sprawling to the ground. His hand kept questing for whatever weapon he had hidden beneath his jacket, but Maya's hand closed around his wrist, locking him in place. She hit him with her free hand, once, then again, feeling the impact jarring up her arm.

He hit back at her, but it was a weak blow with his offhand, one that clipped her skull but didn't come close to stunning her. Maya hit him again, then wrenched his arm. It came out of his jacket holding a squat, ugly revolver.

Now, Maya's full attention was on the weapon. She grabbed Middlen's weapon with both hands, twisting the barrel away from her. She found an opening to hit him with a knee to the stomach, and she heard the whoosh of air leaving his lungs. Maya drove another knee into him to be sure, then turned Middlen's gun with her hand over his, putting it to his own skull.

"Stop fighting," she commanded. "Stop, right now."

Middlen seemed to understand the danger that he was in. He went still.

"Who are you?" he demanded. "You a cop?"

"FBI," Maya replied. "Agent Gray."

She saw the color drain from his face in a way it hadn't simply from having his own weapon pressed to his temple. It seemed that Middlen must have read some of the press coverage that had followed her arrest of the Moonlight Killer.

"Why are you chasing *me* down?" Middlen demanded. Maya twisted the gun from his grasp, holding it on him as she stood and moved back a step, where he couldn't make a grab for it.

"Because Michael Francis Hanratty once paid to stay in one of your storage units," Maya said. "And now he's escaped from prison, I thought he might try the same again. Where is he, Middlen?"

"So you want to look around my unit?" Middlen demanded. "Do you have a warrant, lady?"

"Do you want me to come back with one?" Maya countered. "Because, if I do, then we arrest you for *everything* that you're helping to store. I'm guessing it isn't people's old furniture, is it? And in the meantime, I get impatient with you. Do you *want* me impatient with you?"

Something in her voice must have gotten through to him. Some hint of Maya's desperation to find Hanratty. He couldn't know what she would do to get that information, mostly because Maya didn't fully know how far she would go either.

Middlen hesitated, then finally answered. "Look, he isn't here. He hasn't *been* here. You said it yourself: you know he's used this place. He's not stupid enough to go anywhere you might know."

"Show me anyway," Maya said. She wasn't about to take his word for it.

Middlen led the way back to the storage facility. Maya kept a weapon on him at all times, not trusting him for a moment. They walked inside, and Maya gestured to the first of the containers.

"Open it."

"I don't have the keycards."

Maya gave him a hard look. "You think I believe for one moment that you don't make copies? That you don't make sure you have access if you want it?"

"My clients won't be happy with me," Middlen tried.

"They aren't here. I am."

He sighed and pulled out a keycard, setting it to the electronic lock on the container. It opened, giving Maya a view of crates that might have contained anything from guns to drugs, but there was no sign of Hanratty.

She made him open every storage unit there. The contents would have been enough to keep her department busy for a month, but all Maya felt was a sense of disappointment. There was no sign of Hanratty there, no sign that he'd even been there. There were weapons, drugs, goods that were almost certainly stolen, but there was no sign of the killer.

"See," Middlen said. "Nothing."

Maya knew that she ought to arrest him then, simply for what was in the containers, but the odds of making anything stick were low when she didn't have a warrant. She turned to the door instead.

"You're just going?" Middlen asked.

"You'd rather I arrested you?" Maya retorted. She could call this place in later. She wasn't interested in him, not then. There was only one man Maya was interested in arresting, and for the last two weeks, it had been as if the Moonlight Killer had vanished into thin air.

CHAPTER THREE

"You have a bruise," Megan said.

Maya put a hand to her face self-consciously as she sat out in the backyard of the home she shared with Agent Marco Spinelli. He wasn't home right then, but it seemed that he rarely was, these days. He seemed to take every piece of undercover work the FBI threw his way so that Maya felt as if she barely got to see him.

"Just a perp who got a little out of hand," Maya said. "Nothing major."

"I thought a part of you running a department at a field office was that you didn't have to go out into the field all the time, taking down bad guys?" Megan said.

Megan was Maya's younger sister. She had the same dark hair and eyes, but she was shorter, more delicately built, her features almost fragile. It was what had made her fit the Moonlight Killer's victim profile, a part of what had made him kidnap her, using her and the other women he held to force Maya to investigate cold cases wrongly attributed to him.

Today, Megan was wearing a floral print dress, while Maya was dressed casually, in jeans and a t-shirt. Every moment with Megan was precious, given how close Maya had come to losing her, but even so, right now, at least half of Maya's thoughts were elsewhere, thinking about places Hanratty might have gone to ground.

"Maya, are you even listening to me?" Megan asked, leaning forward on her sun lounger, looking a little concerned. "I was asking what you're doing out in the field."

"Sometimes I miss the action," Maya said. It was a safe response, one that didn't let Megan know how frantically she'd been hunting for the Moonlight Killer in the last couple of weeks.

Megan raised an eyebrow. "Is that really it, or have you been out hunting for… *him*?"

Megan had grown a lot more perceptive since Hanratty took her. Or maybe she just knew how much catching the Moonlight Killer still meant to Maya.

"I was chasing down a lead on him," Maya admitted. "I found a possibility, and I didn't want to risk ignoring it."

She heard Megan sigh. "You should leave that to the rest of the FBI or the Marshals. Aren't they the ones who deal with escaped prisoners?"

Maya could hear the exasperation there, along with a note of something deeper: fear. Megan was afraid. Was she worried that Maya being involved might pull her back into all of this? Maya knew that her sister wanted to try to put everything that had happened to her behind her, and that couldn't be easy when Maya was still hunting for a killer.

"Megan, I probably know him better than anyone else at this point," Maya said. "I have a better chance of tracking him down than the others. More than that, it's obvious that he isn't done playing games with me. Look at what happened with Lucy."

Lucy Barnet was another of the women who had been kidnapped by the Moonlight Killer. She'd been one of those Maya had saved on that last night when she'd raided the bunker where he was keeping them. Yet, she'd been kidnapped again, this time by Administrator Higgins, who ran the secure psychiatric facility Hanratty had been sent to, and who it seemed had come to believe in the Moonlight Killer's so called "mission" to change the world. He'd forced Maya to work another case, exactly the way Hanratty had.

And the whole thing had been set up to keep Maya as far away as possible while Hanratty escaped. Now, both he and Higgins were missing. Maya hadn't been able to find a single sign of either of them. She hated being used like that. She hated the fact that Hanratty could have that kind of power over her.

"You're zoning out again," Megan said, as Maya started to get lost in her thoughts. "Maya, I've told you before that I'm worried about how obsessed you get when it comes to him. How much you get sucked into his games."

"I'm not obsessed," Maya said. "I'm just worried. Worried about what he might do next, worried that we haven't found any traces of him. Worried that he seems to have these *followers* who'll do anything for him. Why would someone want to follow around a serial killer?"

"I don't know, Maya, why would they?" Megan gave her a pointed look.

Maya shook her head, hurt that her sister would make the comparison. "That's not the same. I'm trying to bring him to justice. I'm not doing everything that he wants."

"Aren't you?" Megan countered.

Maya frowned, a little irritated now. "What do you mean?"

"I mean that, from the start of this, he's been as obsessed with you as you seem to be with him. He's spent his time trying to make you do what he wants, trying to get you to run around solving cases for him. And now, you're running around after him, hunting him. Aren't you worried that he's doing the same, trying to work out the best way to get to you?"

Maya wasn't worried about that possibility. If anything, she welcomed it. If Frank Hanratty wanted to try to hunt her even as she hunted him, then let him come. She would take him on, take him down, and not feel a moment of regret about doing it. She'd beaten him before, and she could do it again. If he wanted to come after her, then that would only make it easier.

The worst scenario was that he might simply run, heading to a non-extradition country and disappearing. If he was coming after her, at least that meant that she didn't have to worry about him vanishing to some place where Maya would never find him.

She *was* worried about what else Hanratty might do. Maya wasn't the only one he had unfinished business with. His followers had gone after one of his escaped victims before, after all.

"I know one way he could get to me," Maya said. "If he hurt you. With him out of prison, there's a chance he might target you, might try to kill you or even to kidnap you again."

Megan gave her a level look, not saying anything for several seconds Maya could see a flicker of fear there, but also determination. "Do you think I haven't been thinking about that? That I haven't worried about it every day since he escaped?"

Maya reached out to put a hand on her sister's arm, trying to comfort her, trying to let her know that she was safe.

"Then let me arrange some kind of witness protection for you until he's back behind bars," Maya said. "I can make a call, and you can be somewhere he won't find you within a day. You'll be safe until I can put him back in prison."

To her surprise, though, Megan shook her head. "And how long would that be, Maya? I get the feeling that you and he will be chasing one another around forever in some never-ending dance."

"I can catch him," Maya said. She was determined to do that. She was determined to find him. She wasn't going to let anything stop her from bringing him to justice.

"But maybe it will take you a year to do it," Megan said. "Maybe longer. In that time, I'm meant to go somewhere else, be someone else? I can't do it, Maya. He already took away my life for weeks, stuck in that bunker. I'm not going to volunteer to hide myself away somewhere else. I talked to the others about this. The only way that we win against him is to live our lives, to make the changes that he tried to rob us of."

Maya knew that Hanratty had targeted the women he'd kidnapped right when they'd been on the cusp of major changes in their lives, robbing them of their futures the way war had robbed the other members of his military unity of theirs. In Megan's case, she'd been on the verge of going back to school, giving up her wild partying days.

Under other circumstances, she would have commended the bravery of the freed women trying to go on with their lives, trying not to let what Hanratty had done change them.

Now, though, it just made her worry for all of them. For Megan, in particular. They were all targets now, and Maya knew just how easily a man like Hanratty could get to them.

Maya tried to think of something that she could say that might persuade her sister, that might change Megan's mind, but she knew how strong Megan's will could be now. When she'd made a decision, there was no getting her to go another way.

Maya was still trying to find a way to make Megan agree to some kind of protection when her phone rang. Maya wanted to ignore it, but she couldn't, especially not when she saw Deputy Director Swift's name on the screen.

She picked up, and the other woman's voice came onto the end of the line. Before the capture of the Moonlight Killer, she'd just been Agent Swift, the head of the taskforce trying to capture him. Now, she'd gotten a promotion, but Maya guessed that this was still something personal to her. Something she wasn't about to let go.

"Deputy Director?" Maya said.

"Gray," Swift said without preamble, "how soon can you get into the office?"

"The field office?"

"No," Swift said. "How soon can you get *here*, Gray? To my office at headquarters?"

"Under an hour," Maya said.

"Make it sooner," Swift said, and hung up.

She hadn't given Maya any information about what this was about, but the urgency of the call suggested that something major was happening. There was only one case that connected the two of them: the Moonlight Killer. Was Swift restarting her taskforce? Was she bringing in Maya for her expertise in hunting this singularly dangerous serial killer?

Maya didn't know, but she was determined to find out. She needed to get to the FBI offices.

CHAPTER FOUR

Maya headed into the main building of the FBI headquarters with a sense of trepidation, not knowing what she was doing there, not knowing why Deputy Director Swift might have called her in at such short notice.

Could there be a lead in the Moonlight Killer case? Had they found a location for the fugitive serial killer?

It was the only reason why Maya could imagine Swift bringing her in there, the only real point of connection between them. For months, Maya had been trying to tell Swift that there were at least three unsolved cases out there, because Francis Hanratty had been quite clear in his obsession with twelves. Twelve victims by his hand, twelve more women taken to force Maya to clear his name. Twelve men in his former unit, dead in an operation that the military wasn't about to reveal details of. To Maya, the pattern had been clear.

Especially when Maya had saved three women before Hanratty could use them as bargaining chips in his deadly game. Three women meant three crimes where he'd been planning to force Maya to prove his innocence. It meant three murderers walking around with people thinking that the Moonlight Killer was responsible for their crimes. Maya had caught one of them, but there were still two out there, somewhere.

Maybe Swift had finally come around to her way of thinking and was going to send Maya to search for the truth in those remaining cases. Maybe she just needed Maya's help with the manhunt. The rumor was that the old Moonlight Killer taskforce was being brought back into being.

Maya made her way up, not to the fourth floor and the old Cold Cases unit, but higher now, to the very top floor, where Swift had an office overlooking the city. Maya was surprised to find Marco standing outside that office, looking puzzled, as if he wasn't sure why he was there.

Maya hurried over and put her arms around him. It might be strange that he was there, but Maya was still glad that he was. It felt good not having to keep the two of them being together a secret anymore. She could feel the muscles of Marco's swimmer's body beneath his slightly rumpled dark suit, and he was tall enough that even Maya had to look up to meet his deep blue eyes and take in his boyish good looks. His sandy hair was a mess, as always, but Maya resisted the urge to run her fingers through it. They were at work, after all.

"Marco? I wasn't expecting you here," Maya said, stepping back from him at last. "I thought you were working undercover on a case."

Marco looked serious for a moment. "I was. I got pulled from it to be here on Swift's orders. Didn't even get a chance to head home first. Whatever this is, Swift must want it dealt with in a hurry."

"Do you have any idea what this is about?" Maya asked. She didn't want to walk about how little Marco was home these days, or about the fact that Maya was out in the field office in Baltimore most of the time. It was an old argument between the two of them, and what did it say about their relationship that they already had old arguments?

Marco shook his head. "I didn't get anything beyond Swift demanding that I get here as soon as possible. You?"

Maya shrugged. "The same. I assume it's related to the Moonlight Killer, but beyond that, I can't even guess."

Which meant that there was only one way for them to find out what was going on, and why Deputy Director Swift wanted to see them so urgently. Maya stepped forward, knocking on the door.

"Come in," Swift called out, in a terse voice.

Maya and Marco went inside. The office was pristine in a way that suggested a careful attention to detail, the furnishings modern steel and glass, rather than the cheap office furniture Maya had in her own office. There were a couple of pictures on the wall, both of which looked as if they'd come out of a catalogue to give the space a calm, professional feel. The walls and carpet were Gray, while windows all along one wall gave a view out over DC.

Deputy Director Swift sat behind an elegantly ergonomic desk at the far end of the office, reaching out as Maya and Marco entered the room to close something on the computer screen in front of her. Two files sat on the desk side by side, currently closed.

The deputy director was in her late forties, her blonde hair tied back in a businesslike bun, her makeup minimal and understated. She was wearing a suit an order of magnitude more expensive than anything Maya owned, while her steely blue eyes flicked from Maya to Marco and back. She gestured for the two of them to take a seat on the other side of the desk from her, the movement almost a command.

"Can you guess why you're in here, Gray?" Swift demanded, and there was a hint of anger in her tone that Maya couldn't place.

"Something to do with the Moonlight Killer, I assume," Maya said. Beyond that, she couldn't guess. "I heard that you might be putting your task force back together for the search."

Deputy Director Swift cocked her head to one side. "And you figured that you're so indispensable that I just had to pull you back in from a field office and pull Spinelli from undercover work to go chase him?"

It was obvious from her tone that it wasn't that. Maya had never been sure whether the Deputy Director liked her or not. Maya got the feeling that Swift didn't care about her one way or another, just as long as she produced results. Today, though, there was a hard, unfriendly edge to her expression.

Swift sighed and opened the first file on her desk, turning it towards Maya. There were surveillance photographs inside, and Maya's heart leapt into her mouth as she recognized the storage facility she'd staked out. Her feelings of unease only got worse as she saw herself there, chasing after Philip Middlen down an alley.

"So, how long have you been conducting your own hunt for the Moonlight Killer?" Swift demanded. "I take it that's what this was? We had people watching the storage facility, just in case, but then you showed up, asking questions, holding a suspect at gunpoint, making it certain that Hanratty would never go there."

"He wasn't going to go there anyway," Maya said. "That's one thing I got from Middlen. He's going to avoid anywhere he's been before."

"You didn't answer my question," Swift snapped. "How long have you been conducting your own investigation?"

Maya swallowed back her nerves. "Since he escaped."

Swift nodded. "That tallies with what I've been hearing. You've been blundering around, doing your own thing without coordinating with us, getting in the way of my team. And this latest effort… it isn't acceptable, Gray."

Maya wondered just how much trouble she was about to be in. As the head of a field office, she could, in theory, pick and choose the investigations she worked on. But that didn't mean that she could just get in the way of the Deputy Director's team.

Also, if she was in trouble, why was Marco there? He hadn't played a part in any of this.

Swift drummed her fingers on the desk. "It strikes me that the only useful thing to do now is bring you back onto that team. Both of you."

"Both of us?" Marco said, sounding confused and perhaps a little disappointed.

"What's wrong? Don't want to team up again with your girlfriend?" Swift asked. "Normally, of course the FBI doesn't approve of that kind of thing, but I think that, in this case, you're the best chance we have of reining in Agent Gray's more impulsive moments."

"So, Marco's meant to act as my minder while I hunt for the Moonlight Killer?" Maya said.

Swift shook her head, her expression hard. "Let's be clear, hunting for the Moonlight Killer is *not* your job right now. I already have agents on it. I'm bringing you into the team to stop you getting in the way."

"But-" Maya began.

"What makes you think that I was asking your opinion?" Swift said, cutting her off. "I'm a deputy director of the FBI, and you're going to follow my orders, Agent Gray. You too, Spinelli. I'm bringing you onto the team so that you don't ruin anything else by charging in the way you did with Middlen."

"And what are we actually meant to do?" Marco asked. He didn't sound happy about any of this. Maya guessed that he didn't like being pulled from the investigation he'd been working on.

Swift pushed the second file in Maya's direction. "In spite of everything, the two of you *do* have as much familiarity with the Moonlight Killer's methods as anyone. You know his networks, you know his past. You've looked into so many cases connected to him that I would be an idiot to ignore your expertise. So I'm going to give you this one. A murder that got called in to us from a university in a small town just outside DC: Miltonberg. A professor there, Laura Gibson, was killed a couple of days ago. The local police flagged it as potentially Moonlight Killer related. I suspect that's mostly because it comes so soon after his escape, but we should check it out."

"So, you're sending us in a completely different direction to keep us out of your way?" Maya asked.

Swift's expression held a hint of triumph. "Exactly. Besides, you seem to specialize in cases that *aren't* Hanratty's work, and this seems to fit the bill."

A part of Maya wanted to throw the file back in the deputy director's face, but she knew that would be the quickest way to get fired. In any case, Swift was right. She and Marco had brought a lot of killers to justice in the past year or so. Even if there wasn't a Moonlight Killer connection, a woman had been murdered and she deserved justice.

Maya looked over to Marco, trying to read his expression. He didn't look entirely happy. "Are you okay with this?"

"I'm not sure either of us gets a choice," Marco pointed out.

"You don't," Swift agreed.

Maya took a breath, making sure she didn't say anything she would regret.

"All right," she said at last. "We'll take the case."

CHAPTER FIVE

"I can't believe that Swift is keeping us off the hunt for Hanratty!" Maya complained as Marco drove the two of them over to Miltonberg. "We're her best shot of catching him again."

Marco was silent, staring ahead of himself at the road. He didn't look any happier than he had in Swift's office.

"What is it?" Maya asked him.

He glanced over at her. "Do you really have to ask?"

Maya paused, the case file in her hands. "This is because I was out looking for him, isn't it?"

"You got me pulled from a case, Maya. We were starting to build a life. You were running a whole field office. I was making a difference in organized crime. Now, here we both are, sucked back into the Moonlight Killer case. You didn't even tell me that you were hunting for him."

"When would I have done that?" Maya countered. It was a low blow, but it was also true. Marco had barely been home in the last couple of weeks. As soon as their last case together had finished, he'd been back undercover again.

Marco sighed. "Maya, you have to keep me in the loop on these things. You put yourself in danger, going after Hanratty alone. He almost killed you last time. Can't you see that I'm worried about you? What would have happened if you got close and he ambushed you?"

A part of Maya understood that. She even liked that Marco cared enough to want her to be safe, but she also didn't want anyone to tell her that she had to back off when it came to the Moonlight Killer.

"Marco, I love you, and I love that you want to keep me safe, but please don't ask me to be someone I'm not. I can't leave this alone. I just can't. Not until he's back in prison."

And she didn't tell Marco because she knew that he would try to stop her. She'd needed to do this, and she couldn't let anything, even the man she loved, stop her from bringing in the Moonlight Killer again.

Marco sighed again. "I know, Maya. But now, we're stuck looking into something that has nothing to do with the Moonlight Killer. You don't get to chase him, I'm reassigned, and we're chasing some… what? A copycat?"

"At least we're partners again," Maya said with a faint smile. They hadn't officially been partners since they'd taken Hanratty down the first time. Even on their last case, Marco had only joined her after Maya had already been engaged on the case. Maya had missed working alongside Marco so much that she ached with the loss.

Marco returned the smile, briefly. "There is that. Seriously though, what do we have here?"

Maya turned her attention to the case file. She might not like being put on this case rather than chasing the Moonlight Killer, but now that she was on it, she was determined to do her best to catch the person who had done this. The victim deserved that, deserved her and Marco's best efforts. They couldn't have half their focus on the hunt for Francis Hanratty.

Maya flicked through the file. There wasn't a lot there yet, just sketchy outline details of the crime, a few witness statements taken by the first officers on the scene, a brief profile of the victim.

"Dr. Laura Gibson, 39, was a professor of forensic sciences at the university. She'd written several research papers on elements relating to the recovery of DNA from crime scenes and appeared as an expert witness in a couple of trials. Her students found her two days ago as they came in for their morning lecture with her on DNA comparison techniques. They called in the campus security, who called the local cops, who decided that it looked like a Moonlight Killer case and kicked it to the FBI."

"Cause of death?" Marco asked. He sounded professional now, obviously determined to put his focus into the case.

"I have the coroner's report here," Maya replied. "Let me check."

It was always hard, looking through coroners' reports and crime scene photographs, knowing that the dead body they were discussing had once been a living, breathing human being. That someone had snatched her life away, leaving strangers to poke and prod at the corpse, looking for clues. Maya had looked through so many reports like this in her time working cold cases. Each time, she found herself investing the cold, empty photographs with a sense of who the individual victim had been.

Was it better that the victim had been a professor of forensics? That she would have understood the need for every process had she been alive? Maya wasn't sure that it did, but it did let her feel a kind of kinship with the professor. In her time dealing with cold cases, Maya had spent her days digging into the evidence, trying to find something new, something that could give her a fresh perspective. Often, without people like Dr. Gibson, she wouldn't have been able to do her job at all.

"The coroner puts the cause of death as… blood loss," Maya said, confused for a moment or two, reading on, trying to understand why this had been seen as a Moonlight Killer case.

She saw Marco frown at that, obviously thinking the same thing. "But the locals thought that this was a Moonlight Killer case? Surely everyone knows by now that he strangled his victims?"

Maya looked closer at the report. "The confusion came about because he used a wire garrote," she said at last. "It cut into Dr. Gibson's throat, killing her that way, but it still looked similar."

"Similar enough that someone might have been trying to copy him and made a mistake?" Marco asked.

"Maybe," Maya said. "Although it wasn't a full moon, that's not for at least a week yet. There's something about all this that's familiar, though."

"Familiar how?" Marco asked.

Maya frowned, trying to think as they drove towards the university. Something had snagged in her mind, and she was determined to work out what. They were in Miltonberg now. It looked like a small, prosperous university town there to provide DC with young minds, and maybe a place to commute into the capital from. She could see trees lining the streets on either side, with rows of tall, brownstone houses leading up towards the campus.

"I'm not sure yet. There's something about this location that feels familiar."

"It will come to you. Did they get anything from witnesses at the scene?" Marco asked.

Maya read through the reports quickly, trying to extract any information that might be useful, checking the witness statements, trying to find anything that might be useful.

"As far as I can tell, all the witnesses are just kids who found the body. There's a note from one of her colleagues about stepping in to see her around six last night, and Laura saying that she was going to work late to prepare for the lecture. Other than that, no one saw her until they found her."

"Is there security footage?" Marco said.

That was an obvious potential source of evidence, but there didn't seem to be anything that Maya could see.

"You'd think so, with a university campus, but there's no notes about it in the file," Maya said. "We'll have to ask the campus security when we get there, and-"

Maya happened to glance up then. From the window of the car, she saw the expanse of a public park near the university. On a bright day like this, there were people jogging, a couple of kids playing catch, a few vendors selling hot dogs and ice cream. It was a pretty spot, but that wasn't what caught her attention.

"Stop the car!" Maya said.

Marco didn't stop in the middle of the street, but he did pull over straight away. Maya all but leapt out of the car, starting towards the park, trying to get a better look.

"Maya, what is it?" Marco asked. "What have you seen?"

"Is that Hain Park?" Maya asked.

"Where? I... don't know," Marco admitted. "It's not like I've been to Miltonberg before, Maya. Hold on, I'll check."

He got out his phone, obviously checking their location. He looked up with a certain amount of surprise. "You're right, that is indeed Hain Park. How did you know? Is it somewhere you've been before?"

Maya shook her head. She hadn't been there, but it was a location she'd read about over and over, a location she knew almost perfectly. She'd read reports about it, seen pictures of it, looked over maps of the place. The one thing she hadn't known was just how close it was to the university here in Miltonberg.

"Hain Park is the location where the Moonlight Killer supposedly left Anita Lane, one of the fifteen victims he was convicted for killing," she said.

She saw Marco's eyes widen in surprise. He hadn't gone into the details of Francis Hanratty's kills the way Maya had, trying to find any detail that didn't fit, any reason to discount the kill as one of his.

"So you're saying... what? That there's a Moonlight Killer connection after all?" Marco asked.

It was a logical inference from the location, but Maya still wasn't sure.

"I'm not sure," Maya admitted. She was still trying to process the implications of it all. "I don't think it means that this murder is down to him. The difference in the M.O. is too great. So maybe it's a copycat who's deliberately picked a location close by? Maybe it's someone trying to make it *look* like a Moonlight Killer victim, to deflect attention from themselves? There's even a chance that the first kill is one of the ones that he was going to make me look into."

"But we have no way of knowing that for sure," Marco guessed.

Maya shook her head. "Not without finding him to ask him."

"Then we focus on the murder in front of us," Marco said. "We go to the crime scene, we try to work out who did it, and when we find them, maybe *then* the Moonlight Killer connection will make more sense."

Maya nodded. She knew that Marco was right. It was just that, suddenly, it seemed that there was a whole dimension to this death that she hadn't considered before.

CHAPTER SIX

Maya stood in the middle of the college campus, trying to work out how something as violent as murder could have happened in a place so seemingly peaceful and quiet.

Around her stood ivy-covered buildings, with statues here and there dedicated to major donors to the university, or perhaps famous alumni; Maya didn't stop to find out which. She saw students hurrying between classes or making their way to the library. Most of them seemed to be moving quickly with their heads down, glancing around nervously from time to time as if worried that someone might be lurking nearby. The whole university seemed tense, as if waiting to see if more violence might be about to ensue. Maya was a little surprised that classes weren't cancelled, but it seemed that the university thought that it was still safe for the students, at least.

Maya guessed that the whole quiet and oppressive atmosphere was due to the news of the murder. In a few days or weeks, probably the campus would be back to normal, but only if she and Marco managed to catch whoever had killed Laura Gibson.

"I think the building we want is this way," Marco said, consulting a large map of the campus. The two of them made their way over, watching the students pass by. Several of them stared their way. It was obvious that Maya and Marco stood out on campus. Presumably, it wouldn't be long before the news started to spread that the FBI were there.

At least one person definitely seemed to recognize them for what they were. A white-haired, older man in a pinstripe suit came up to them, looking them up and down with clear blue eyes as if trying to decide if they could really be who he thought they were.

"Are you the FBI?" he asked after a second or two of such consideration.

Maya nodded. "I'm Agent Gray. This is Agent Spinelli. And you are?"

"Oh, yes, forgive me, of course. I am Prof. Walter Nieman. I lecture in criminology here. I heard what happened to dear Laura. I must say,

I'm glad that the FBI are here. Frankly, I'm not confident in the local police department's capacity to do the job when it's something like this."

"Well, we'll do everything we can," Maya assured him. She didn't want to pre-judge the local PD's abilities. She hoped that they might be both willing and able to provide assistance if she and Marco needed it.

"I'm sure. And if you need any help, don't hesitate to ask. I have a couple of grad students who would give their right arms to get in on some real law enforcement work. At least one of them is thinking of applying for the FBI, you know."

"I'm sure they'll fit right in," Marco said, in a non-committal tone. "Excuse us, Prof. Niemann, we need to get going."

"Oh, yes, of course," the older professor said. "The sooner you're done, the sooner we get our building back for lectures."

He wandered off, leaving Maya to wonder if he really thought that the FBI would simply draft in grad students to do the grunt work. Even ones who were planning on applying. Maya smiled at that thought.

"Come on," she said to Marco. "You heard him, we need to get finished so they can use their lecture theater again."

They made their way to a building tucked away behind some of the others, with an ugly, brutalist architectural style that suggested it had been built in the 1960s and then never touched. Maya knew that they'd found the right place when she saw a muscular young man with buzz cut dark hair in the uniform of the local PD at the door, turning people away. Currently, they seemed to be arguing with a petite woman of around forty, with a blond bob hairstyle, wearing dark slacks and a cream sweatshirt under a denim jacket.

"What happened to freedom of the press, Bryant?" the woman demanded, holding a digital recorder out as if expecting some kind of usable quote in response. "Why are you trampling over my First Amendment rights?"

"I've told you before, Ms. Franklin, you're free to *write* what you want, but that doesn't mean that you're free to *go* where you want. Particularly not when that means walking into a crime scene."

"How am I meant to get the full story from out here?" the woman, the reporter, demanded.

"That's not my problem," the officer said, in a calming voice. "All I know is that nobody gets in there until the FBI arrives. The chief wants us to preserve the scene."

Maya chose that moment to walk up, holding her badge out for the guard to see. "Agent Maya Gray, FBI. This is my partner, Agent Marco Spinelli."

It was still strange introducing him that way. For so much of the time they'd worked together, he'd been a Cleveland robbery/homicide detective consulting with the FBI. The moment when he'd passed the training to become a full agent had been one of the proudest of Maya's life.

The guard looked Maya up and down. Sadly, so did the reporter.

"Lisa Franklin, Miltonberg News. Do you have any comment for our readers on this tragic death?"

Maya shook her head. "We only just arrived here, Ms. Franklin."

"But do you think this is the work of the Moonlight Killer?" the reporter asked, clearly not willing to give up. "Is that why they brought *you* in? Maya Gray, the woman who took him down the first time?"

She sounded excited as she said it. Was Maya's involvement in this case really that big a story? Maya still wasn't used to the fact that people knew who she was now; that, since she'd taken down the Moonlight Killer the first time, she'd achieved a level of something like fame.

"We're not ruling anything out at this stage," Marco said, moving to block the reporter's way as she started to edge towards the door to the building. "But for now, we have a job to do. Please let us do it."

"At least let me give you my card," Lisa Franklin said. "If you hear anything, tell me, rather than one of the big networks. The people of Miltonberg deserve to hear about what's happening from a source that cares about their community. From someone *local*."

She held out a card with a determined expression that suggested that she wasn't going to take no for an answer. Since it seemed like the best way to cut their interaction short, Maya took it and tucked it away in the pocket of her jacket.

"If we decide to talk to the press, you'll be the first name I think of," Maya said. Not that she had any intention of talking to the media on this case. The last thing she wanted was to fuel fears about what might be happening in the town.

She and Marco slipped into the building, the campus security guard following them, pointedly closing the doors to keep out Lisa Franklin and locking them.

"Sorry about her," he said. "She's been pestering us for access pretty much from the moment this started. Heck, I think she got here before we did. She was already here, arguing with campus security, when we arrived."

"You're... Bryant?" Maya said, recalling the name Lisa had used.

"That's right," the officer replied. "The local department has been coordinating campus security to watch this place in shifts since it happened, making sure everything was secure. We knew the FBI would want to look things over without a bunch of students walking through it."

"Thank you," Maya replied. They were currently walking along a long corridor, which gave no clues to where it led. Noticeboards on either side proclaimed everything from a meeting of the student science society to the date of a major academic conference.

"When there aren't guards around, what would access to the building be like?" Marco asked. He was obviously thinking about how the killer had gotten in.

Bryant shrugged. "Pretty easy, I guess. The place is unlocked in the day. After hours, there's a keycard system, but from what I understand, a lot of people have them, and they lose them all the time. You know what students are like. Not to mention the more forgetful older academics."

Meaning that it wouldn't necessarily help to track who had accessed the building when. Even so, Maya decided that it might be worth a shot.

"We're going to need details of which cards accessed the building on the night Laura Gibson died," she said. "Is there security footage too? There wasn't any mention of it in the file."

Bryant nodded. "The guards gave us copies. We didn't find anything obvious, but if you want, you can come into the security room and take a look. With the older buildings like this, there are plenty of blind spots, though, and one of the cameras hasn't been working for a couple of weeks."

Meaning that it might potentially have been easy for the killer to avoid being spotted if they knew where the cameras were. The timing was interesting. Had they broken the camera, taken advantage of it being down, or merely gotten lucky?

"Here you go," Bryant said as they reached a set of double doors sealed by police tape. He opened them, revealing a large lecture theater within, small windows high above letting in light to filter down onto rows of seats below.

"Were you one of the first cops on the scene?" Marco asked.

Bryant nodded. He looked troubled. "I remember seeing her there. Of course, by that point, there were students all around, half of them with their phones out. The security guards were trying to keep them back, but I get the feeling they didn't know what to do. We had to push them all back before we could do anything."

With so many people so close to the body, it probably meant that the police's forensics wouldn't be that useful. They would get far too many samples, the whole scene contaminated before it could be properly contained.

"Were the lights on when you got in there?" Maya asked, looking at the banks of lights embedded in the ceiling. They were currently dark, the natural sunlight above providing more than enough illumination for the scene. "Did anyone turn them off later?"

Bryant shook his head. "I don't think so. I certainly don't remember anyone turning them off."

"You think that might be significant?" Marco asked.

"I'm just trying to get a sense of how this happened," Maya said. "Where was the body?"

Bryant gestured to the front of the lecture theater, where the remains of a bloodstain marred the lectern there. Yet Maya could see more bloodstains further up, dots of blood, with a larger pool closer to the entrance, maybe halfway up the stairs. She crouched by that stain, taking pictures for evidence, trying to understand what had happened.

"She was found down there, but there are blood stains here," Maya said.

"You think she was killed here and then dragged back to display her better?" Marco asked.

Maya nodded, but in one way, that didn't make a lot of sense. "That doesn't fit the Moonlight Killer's pattern. If this guy were trying to copy him, surely, he would know that Hanratty leaves his victims without posing them?"

"So, this isn't about copying him?" Marco said.

Maya wasn't sure. She gestured to the lecture theater. "And look at this place. It's not a great spot to try to kill someone. It would be a lot easier in one of the corridors, just leap out from behind an office door and you have an easy ambush. This, it's almost as if he wanted her to know that death was coming."

"He wanted her to run and to be able to kill her anyway," Marco said.

Maya looked around, imagining how it must have gone. Had the killer followed Laura into the lecture theater and killed her on her way down to the front? No, that didn’t work, because there were forensic notes written on the boards down by the lectern, and the police report on the crime scene said that notes had been taken from the lectern as evidence. She must have made it there before she died.

She'd been at the front, and he'd managed to sneak in. He'd startled her and somehow managed to get behind her. The fact that the lights hadn't been on when Bryant got there suggested that he'd killed the lights to give him a better chance of getting to her without being spotted. He'd spooked Laura into trying to run, then killed her while she did it. After that, he'd dragged her back to the lectern to leave her where her students would find her.

“Whoever did this planned this, but there’s nothing clinical about this,” Maya said. “This is someone who cares about the thrill of the hunt at least as much as the kill. Someone who wants to hurt his victims, not just kill them quickly.”

“That’s definitely not the Moonlight Killer,” Marco said.

Maya nodded, confirming it. No, they were dealing with a very different kind of monster here indeed.

CHAPTER SEVEN

The man they called Frank watched his latest two followers with amusement, as he sat on the fringes of his latest hiding place, watching them load boxes into a small van.

There was a man there and a woman, a couple, judging by the way they looked at one another. The man was scrawny, brown haired and average looking, the woman a little prettier and blonde haired, although without the delicate fragility that might have made her interesting in the ways that mattered. That might have made her prey, not an assistant. They had names, of course, but Frank was careful not to use them, even in the privacy of his head. It was better to keep good discipline, even there.

It amused him the way the two of them looked at one another. The man looked over to the woman every so often with obvious desire, but only when he was sure that she wasn't looking, as if he feared her reaction if she caught him. When she *was* looking, he looked at her with worry, even fear. He followed her instructions to the letter, flinching when she raised her voice. For her part, she looked at the man mostly with contempt, as well as with a cold calculation, as if wondering if he might be more use to her dead.

Frank idly wondered which of them would kill the other first. Would fear or contempt be the greater driving force.

It had come as something of a surprise to him to learn that he had acolytes now. Oh, he'd always had helpers, but those had been people he'd paid and carefully kept at a distance. People he could use and discard, without them ever having real contact with him.

Yet it seemed that he'd also built up something different, too. People who were prepared to do what he wanted, not because Frank threatened or bribed them, but because they *wanted* to. Because they *believed* in him.

Frank was careful to keep the disgust he felt at that thought off his face. It was a handsome face, in a forgettable kind of way, close to forty, square jawed and with his dark hair cropped close. He was athletic and strong, the kind of man who might have attracted attention in a bar if he wanted it, at least until anyone looked into his eyes and saw the coldness there.

But Frank could hide that, when he wanted to do so. He could be charismatic, manipulative, even charming when the situation called for it. It was just one of the skills his time in the military had taught him: how to find the levers that made people work. How to pull on those levers until they believed that they were making their own choices about what to do, all the while doing exactly what Frank wanted.

And now, it seemed, he had more levers to pull than ever. He had notoriety, had whole legions of writers, reporters and others speculating over what the point of his kills had been, what his goals were. He'd heard them discussing the way he took his victims on the very cusp of change as if it were almost an article of religious faith. His success as a killer had made ordinary people fear him, but to a certain kind of person, it seemed that it also made him into something else: an inspirational figure, a leader. To some of them, something close to a god.

That was something that Frank could use to achieve what he needed to achieve.

"Is everything ready?" Frank asked, standing and heading over to the van. He took care to move without showing pain, even though the spot where Maya Gray had shot him in the leg ached with every movement. Some things never healed quite correctly.

"We'll have everything in place by tonight," the woman said. "And in return…"

She held out a hand expectantly. Frank smiled at that, at the fact that even now, there was a kind of exchange involved in these transactions. It seemed that not everyone loved him that much. Some people weren't capable of it.

"As agreed," Frank said, taking out a scrap of paper. The contents were nothing important to him, merely details of how the two before him could undertake one of their own hunts, how they could get to the victim they'd picked out. How they could avoid leaving any trace when they'd had their fun. Frank liked to think that he was providing a valuable service. "And of course, you wouldn't dream of failing to fulfill your part of the bargain."

The woman raised an eyebrow. "And look over my shoulder every full moon? We'll do what we promised."

Frank watched them leave. He headed back inside, then down, into the bunker that Administrator Higgins had so carefully constructed for him. As if the thought had summoned him, the former hospital administrator ran forward, tall and muscled, dressed all in black as if in imitation of Frank when he went out searching for a kill. Of course, Frank didn't dress like that the rest of the time, preferring simple, casual clothes that wouldn't draw attention. It wasn't a *costume* to him, the way it was for the administrator.

"Did everything go okay?" the administrator asked. "Is everything going the way you planned?"

The fervor of an acolyte, or perhaps an overeager puppy. This was the man who had helped to break Frank out of a secure psychiatric facility, because it turned out that Administrator Higgins had his own dark thoughts that had merely needed to be shaped, given purpose. Given an outlet. Frank had been able to work with that, to shape it to his own ends.

"Everything is running smoothly," Frank said. "Tell me, what's the latest on Maya Gray?"

"Why do you bother with her?" the other man demanded, his voice a whine. "Why do you care so much about her, when-"

Frank jabbed him in the throat in one swift movement. Not hard. Not hard enough to break the trachea or smash the hyoid bone, at any rate. But hard enough to leave the former administrator gasping for air, backing away from Frank, the fear on his features obvious.

Not everyone who wanted to be a predator *was* one. Some people felt far too much for that. Frank didn't care. To Frank, people like this were just another tool to use.

"You do not ask questions about Maya," Frank said. He didn't need to raise his voice, not with a man like this. It was better to show that he could hurt him while being perfectly, icily calm. "You answer them. Now, while you get your breath back, I want you to think about what will happen if the next words out of your mouth don't tell me where she is and what she's doing. You *have* been monitoring her the way I showed you, right?"

Administrator Higgins nodded, still gasping for air. "She… she's in a place called Miltonberg."

That news was enough to make Frank smile. Better and better. If she was there, it could only mean one thing. Plus, it meant that she was a long way away from his current location and where he intended to go next. It would give him time in which to set up everything he needed to do. It was important to keep moving, and Maya Gray had proven herself to be the one person able to keep up with him.

He had someone in Miltonberg. He would be able to get all the updates he needed.

Frank fantasized about what it would be like to kill Maya. She would be the hardest prey he'd ever taken down, a woman who would kill him in return if he put even one foot wrong. For now, she had a job to do, clearing his name of another of the murders falsely attributed to him, another distraction, taking attention away from the true beauty of the pattern he'd wrought.

She would do that, he was sure of it. Although Frank had generally found that she worked best with suitable stakes on the line, he had to admit that she could be quite resourceful even under her own direction.

Frank returned his attention to the administrator. Probably, Frank would have to kill *him* at some point, too. Frank always found it best to decide when he met people what the easiest way to kill them would be, in case it ever came up. In Administrator Higgins' case, it would be a lot easier than with Maya Gray.

"Get everything ready," Frank instructed. "We'll move on in an hour."

They would move on to his next hiding place, and then… well, Frank had one more plan to put in motion. A plan that would be the culmination of everything that he'd done so far.

CHAPTER EIGHT

"This is hopeless."

The security footage wasn't getting them anywhere. Maya sat in the campus's security room, drinking coffee that had come from a vending machine down the hall and looking at one of a bank of screens that seemingly let campus security see everything that was going on in the college at once.

Maya was scrolling through footage on one screen, while Marco worked on another. Bryant was standing close by as if waiting to find out what else he could do to help.

"It's a nice setup they have here," Marco observed. "But I'm struggling to get a sense of exactly where the cameras are placed."

"You should be able to pull up a campus map with them on," Bryant said. "Here."

He leaned over and hit a few keys. Sure enough, a map came up on one of the screens. It showed camera locations, along with the fields of vision for those cameras, represented by slowly rotating segments of lighter Gray on the map.

"Could someone get in here and see this map?" Maya asked, trying to work out what resources the killer might have had. Trying to work out *who* might have had those resources.

"I don't know," Bryant said. "Maybe if they said that there was a security problem and they needed to look back through the footage."

Maybe they wouldn't even need to. Maybe they could just make notes of the camera positions. Maya could see that one of the cameras near the lecture theater was flagged as broken, just as Bryant had said. The question now was whether that would be enough to let the killer in without being spotted.

"Okay," she said. "I'm going to test whether the killer really could have gotten there without being tracked by any cameras."

"You want me to see if you appear on screen?" Marco said.

Maya smiled. "Make sure you catch my good side. Bryant, I'll need to borrow a keycard for the building."

The cop grabbed one from a pile and handed it over without arguing, which might just have been because Maya was FBI and he knew what she had planned, but it also confirmed what he'd said about keycard security not being that tight around campus.

She slipped out of the security room, calculating her route. It looked tight, even with the broken camera. It was also important to be able to do this without looking obvious to anyone passing by, because the killer wouldn't have been able to be certain that there would be no one walking past even in the quiet of the night.

Maya started to make her way along the route she'd picked out, deliberately starting at the library, since it struck her as a place where the killer could afford to be seen by a camera without it seeming suspicious. They would seem like just one more student or staff member heading out after an evening of research. Maya stood out now, but there was no reason to think that the killer would have.

Maya started to make her way along the route she'd picked out, moving carefully, knowing that her margin of error was relatively low. She had to move over to edge along one of the walls at one point, but it wasn't in full view of the main plaza of the campus, so it was plausible. She had to pause in one spot, waiting for a camera to turn the other way, then hurry out from underneath it to the next part of her route. The broken camera was near one of the entrances, which meant that Maya could make her way inside the building.

Now, she didn't have to worry about moving in an unobtrusive fashion. She could duck under the field of vision of one camera, cut straight through a classroom and keep going. She picked her way slowly forward, finally coming to the door of the lecture theater. Maya reversed her route then, heading back along the same path that she'd used to get there. It took several minutes to get back to the security room, but when she got there, Marco and Bryant were still staring at the screens.

"Anything?" Maya asked. Bryant jumped slightly in his seat, while Marco didn't seem startled in the slightest.

"You made it to the lecture theater and back?" Marco replied, raising an eyebrow.

Maya nodded. "In broad daylight, and it would have been easier in the dark."

"Which explains why we can't find anything in the security footage for the night Dr. Gibson died," Marco said. "But it also means that we're not looking for a killer with some kind of special security access or the capacity to change the footage."

Maya didn't know whether to feel disappointment that they weren't going to get any evidence that way or satisfaction that she'd probably found the route the killer had taken. Probably the former, since she didn't see how knowing the route was going to lead her and Marco back to the killer. Maybe it implied an insider, used to the university grounds, but anyone who managed to spend time there might be able to slowly pick up the security layout.

"Do you need anything else here from me?" Bryant asked.

"Actually, yes," Maya said. "Can you start looking through security footage around the library for the night Laura Gibson died? Make a note of anyone who stands out to you, anyone who doesn't seem familiar, or who seems to be behaving strangely?"

"That could be a long list," Bryant pointed out.

Maya nodded. "I know, but maybe there will be something in there that we can use."

"And can we tell the college they can have their building back?" Bryant asked. "The university authorities don't like having the whole building out of use like this."

Maya looked over to Marco, who shrugged.

"I think we've gotten everything we're going to get from the crime scene," he said.

Maya could only agree with that, however frustrating it was to do so.

"Yes," she said. She handed Bryant a card. "We've seen everything we're going to see there. Thank you, Bryant. If you find anything in the footage, call us."

Maya and Marco left Bryant in the security room, heading out into the open air of the campus.

"What now?" Marco asked. It was a good question because they seemed to have exhausted all their immediate options. The evidence around the crime scene wasn't going to lead them straight to the killer, so they were going to have to start digging into Laura Gibson's life and career, trying to find out who might have had a reason to want to kill her.

Maya was about to suggest that when a man came running up to them. He was in his forties, with a short, dark beard and dark hair that fell down to his shoulders. He was wearing slacks and a sweater, carrying a bag that seemed to be stuffed full with a laptop and papers.

He had a book under one arm. Maya guessed that he might be a lecturer there, but she was more interested in his expression, which was frantic with worry.

"Are you the FBI?" he asked as he hurried over.

"That's right," Maya said. "I'm Agent Gray, this is Agent Spinelli. Who are you?"

"I'm Maxim Hart. I work in the library here." Maya could see him shifting his weight from foot to foot nervously, as if he couldn't stay in one spot for more than a second or two.

"Is something wrong, Mr. Hart?" Marco asked, in a sympathetic tone. He'd obviously seen the same nervousness that Maya had.

"It's my wife," Maxim said. "She's gone missing!"

Maya held up a hand to slow him down. "Okay, try to stay calm. Let's go sit down for a moment."

She led the way over to a bench on campus, sitting down next to Maxim Hart, trying to gauge as she did it just how serious this man was. Was this just someone who had heard the news that a lecturer had died and who was now panicking because his wife wasn't where he expected she would be, or was this something more serious? Even if she *was* missing, was there any connection to the case, or was this something that might be handled better by campus security or the local police?

"What's your wife's name?" Maya asked.

"Evelyn. Evelyn Hart."

"And when did you notice that she'd gone missing?" Marco put in, standing close to the two of them.

"I woke up this morning and found her gone," Maxim said. "That's normal, she often goes out running while I'm still asleep. But we were meant to meet up an hour ago for lunch once she'd finished her morning lectures. She hasn't been answering her phone, and none of her colleagues have seen her all day."

Maya frowned at that. An hour didn't necessarily mean anything, but if her colleagues hadn't seen her, that might mean more.

"Her colleagues?" Maya said. "She's a lecturer here?"

Maxim nodded. "She teaches in the psychology department, specializing in criminal psychology."

Those last two words caught Maya's attention. Was it a coincidence that a lecturer in forensics had been killed, and now a professor of criminal psychology was missing?

“We’ll look into it,” Maya said. “We’ll do everything we can to find her.”

CHAPTER NINE

"Would the university's system let us trace a particular keycard?" Maya asked, without preamble, as she and Marco hurried back into the security office. She needed to know if they could find Evelyn Hart that way.

"Agents, you're back so soon?" Bryant said as Maya and Marco hurried back into the security office. The cop was still there, working through the footage.

"The keycard?" Maya repeated. "Could we trace one?"

Bryant frowned. "I'm pretty sure that there's no keycard evidence close to the time that Dr. Gibson was killed."

"This is something else," Maya said. "We're trying to locate a professor here, Evelyn Hart. Can you track her keycard? We think that she might be in danger."

"*Do* we think that?" Marco asked. "I can see why Maxim Hart is worried, but none of this necessarily means that she's in danger."

Maya felt certain that she was, though. "Maybe it's nothing, but she teaches criminal psychology. A forensics expert and a criminal psychologist? It feels like they're too close in terms of their fields of expertise for this to be a coincidence. If we're lucky, we'll find her alive and well in under an hour and get back to the Laura Gibson case."

"But you don't think that we will?" Marco said.

Maya shook her head. She could feel a sense of dread building inside her, somewhere in the pit of her stomach. She hoped that Evelyn Hart was alive and well, that she'd just gone off with a friend and turned her phone off, or that she'd chosen today of all days to leave her husband without telling him.

But she needed confirmation of that before she could believe it. Right now, her thoughts were turning in a much darker direction, one that she hoped she was wrong about.

"I'll check," Bryant said. He worked on the computer for a few seconds. Maya saw Evelyn's name come up on the screen, then an image of the campus grounds, with a list of times that she'd used her keycard in different spots.

"There's nothing more recent than yesterday," Marco said. Now he sounded a little worried, like he was starting to believe that this might be more than someone leaving town suddenly.

Maya was getting more worried by the second. "So, that means that she didn't come in to work today. She went out for her run, or said that she did, and then never got here."

"It's still possible that this isn't connected," Marco said, but now even he didn't sound like he really believed it. "She could have gone for a run, tripped and ended up in the hospital."

"Without her husband being called?" Maya said.

"Or she could have lied to him about going for a run in order to leave him, run off with some secret lover or something," Marco suggested. It matched the thought that Maya had had before, but she still didn't think it was the real explanation.

Even so, she knew that they had to check.

"You call the hospital," she said. "I'll find a cell phone number for Evelyn and try that."

"There should be one on file with the college administration," Bryant said. "I can probably get it for you."

He quickly dug it out of he college's system and Maya put the number into her phone, hoping that Evelyn would pick up, hoping that this would all prove to be nothing after all.

The phone went straight to voicemail, though.

"Evelyn, this is Maya Gray, with the FBI," Maya said. "When you get this, please contact me. I need to confirm that you're safe."

Maya hung up and turned to Marco, who was already shaking his head. "There's no one matching her name in the local hospital."

Which meant that, until they heard otherwise, they had to treat this disappearance as suspicious.

"All right," Maya said. "We need to contact the local police and get them to search for her. I'll send a message through to the techs at the FBI and get them to flag any phone use with a location. I'll ask them to track credit card use as well."

"Bryant, you'll need to call this in," Marco said.

"You really think that she's in danger, don't you?" Bryant said.

Maya nodded. "Her going missing so soon after Laura Gibson's death is suspicious. Working in linked fields like that, there's a chance that the two knew one another, that this disappearance could be connected."

If so, the question was whether Evelyn was another potential victim or perhaps a potential suspect. Was it possible that she'd run once she'd heard that the FBI were being called in to investigate the death? Or had someone killed Evelyn for the same reason that they'd killed Laura?

Maya sent the message, getting a confirmation back that the number was now being tracked. She needed to think of other ways of finding her now. She probably needed to go back to Maxim Hart and ask him about places she might go, people she knew. She needed to ask if there was anyone who might mean her harm.

For the moment, though, Maya needed to think about the killer, about the potential worst case scenario here. If she assumed for a second that something had happened to Evelyn, that the same killer had targeted her, then why did no one know about it yet? Laura's murder had been deliberately staged, her body placed so that she would be found in as public a way as possible. If the killer wanted his victims found, then why hadn't Maya received a call yet saying that there was a body?

She also thought about the link in this town to the Moonlight Killer cases, to one of the ones for which Francis Hanratty had been convicted. Maya found herself thinking about Hain Park then, about its wide open spaces and the people who were using it. Where would someone go running near the university if not there?

A cold thread of certainty started to run through Maya. She knew, or at least thought she knew, where Evelyn Hart was. She turned to Marco.

"Marco, we need to get to Hain Park," she said. "Bryant, ask the local cops to get a unit there. If I'm right, we're going to need their help."

***

The park was quiet and bright as Maya and Marco pulled up in front of its gates. There were still families out there, one even having a picnic on the grass, but the whole place seemed too peaceful for what Maya suspected.

"So, you think that the killer might have killed Evelyn and left her in the park?" Marco said.

"Not just anywhere in the park," Maya replied. She pulled up the file on her phone. "If he's copying the Moonlight Killer, doesn't the spot where the Moonlight Killer murdered someone make sense as a place to check?"

Marco nodded. "I just hope that you're wrong."

"So do I," Maya agreed.

The two of them got out of the car and headed into the park. They moved along one of the paths there, with Maya using her notes on the much older crime as a guide.

"There should be a stand of trees somewhere ahead," she said. She looked around until she saw one that looked likely. A side branch of the path went through there, and Maya set off along it.

"You're sure you can find the precise spot?" Marco said. He seemed to think for a moment. "Would the *killer* be able to find it?"

Maya was confident that she could, at least. "I've stared at the files for so long, I'm confident that I can find it. As for the killer… the information is publicly available at this point. So many articles and books have been written about the Moonlight Killer by now that you can find out almost anything about him."

"Making it easy to copy his kills," Marco said, with a note of disgust.

Maya nodded. The two of them kept moving along the tree lined path, their shade cutting out much of the light from above, turning the stand of trees into a place of shadows and flickering glimpses of the sky above. It felt oppressive in there, although that might have been the thought of what they might be walking towards. Maya tried to steel herself, but she knew that there were some things it was impossible to prepare for.

Finally, they came out into a clearing with a twisted, dead tree at the center, one that had been carved by so many different hands that it seemed like a work of art. Maya stared at it, and at the figure sitting unmoving at its base.

It was a woman with short auburn hair and angular features. She was dressed in running clothes and sneakers, while her green eyes stared sightlessly at the world beyond. Blood was pooled around her, already dry, while Maya could still see the shine of the wire garotte at her throat. The stench of death filled the air, making Maya have to fight to hold down the rising wave of horror that threatened to overwhelm her at the sight.

For a moment, it was as if she were looking at one of the crime scene photographs from that original case, staring at Francis Hanratty's work, or that of someone trying to make it look like his work.

They'd found Evelyn Hart.

CHAPTER TEN

"Agents, is it true that another woman has been killed?"

Maya flinched at the sound of the reporter's voice coming through the trees. She turned and saw Lisa Franklin approaching, expression determined, almost excited, with her phone held out before her to record. It had only been minutes since they'd found Evelyn Hart, and yet the reporter was here already. How was she doing it?

"I'm going to have to ask you to clear the area, Ms. Franklin," Maya said.

"Is it Evelyn Hart? The woman they've been saying is missing?"

Maya frowned at that. "How do you know that?"

The journalist smiled slightly. "I have my sources. Can you confirm whether this is connected to the Moonlight Killer murders? Has Michael Francis Hanratty started killing again since he escaped?"

"We don't believe at this time that he is involved," Maya said.

Marco was approaching from the journalist's other side. "This is a crime scene, Ms. Franklin. Clear the area. You could be contaminating evidence."

"All right, all right," Lisa said, backing up. "But would you at least answer a few questions later?"

Maya didn't answer that. Instead, she waited for the journalist to back up further. She could hear the sirens that heralded the arrival of the backup they would need to secure the scene. She was grateful to see uniformed police officers coming through the small stand of woodland.

"How did the press get here before the local cops?" Maya asked.

Marco shrugged. "I guess she has a contact on the force or something. For now, we have to focus on this." He turned his attention to the police officers arriving. "We have a dead female here, killed the same way Laura Gibson was. Spread out and secure the scene, note anything you find. An FBI forensic team is on the way."

Maya watched the police bustling around the crime scene, grateful that she wouldn't have to keep back the onlookers something like this would inevitably draw. Instead, she started to walk the crime scene, looking for any traces that might give her and Marco more information.

Maya found her eye drawn by marks on the ground near the body of Evelyn Hart, leading away from her.

"Look at this," Maya called out to Marco, who hurried over.

"Drag marks?" Marco said.

"Exactly, and blood stains. Evelyn wasn't killed in this spot." Maya photographed the marks quickly, then started to follow them back, tracking them through the trees. She saw a broken branch where someone had pushed it aside. She followed it all the way to a path near the trees, seeing more bloodstains.

"So, the killer attacked her here while she was running, then dragged her back into the trees," Marco said. "I'll get forensics to check this spot too. The local cops can canvas the park to see if anyone saw anything, and the coroner's people will be on the scene for the body."

Maya nodded. That was good. She started to search the area around the path, checking for any evidence that might point to the killer, anything that might have fallen during the initial struggle. She quickly came up empty, though. It seemed that the killer had been careful.

"If there's anything from forensics, it will take time to come through," Marco said. "Do you want to wait here to see what the coroner has to say?"

Maya suspected that they wouldn't be able to tell the two of them much right away, beyond perhaps confirming that the method of murder was the same.

"It's better if we head back to the college," she said. "We need to talk to Laura and Evelyn's colleagues to try to find out if there was anyone with a grudge against them both. Someone who might copy the Moonlight killer to try to cover his tracks."

"Plus, we also need to break the news to Maxim Hart," Marco said.

Maya winced at the thought of having to do that. It was one part of the job that she didn't do much. Usually, by the time she got to a cold case, families had not only been informed, but had also had time to grieve. There was no avoiding the task of telling Evelyn's husband here, though. They had to do it before he found out another way.

"Come on, we need to get back to the college," Maya said.

The two of them headed back to the car, then drove over to the college. As they drove, Maya thought about the way this case seemed to be connected more strongly than anyone thought to the Moonlight Killer's cases. Swift had sent them here to keep them out of the way, yet now it seemed that this whole thing might be linked after all.

It was a short walk to the library, where Maxim Hart worked, but with every step, Maya felt her dread of the conversation she had to have next growing. She'd seen how much a murder could change the lives of families, how much it could rip apart whatever stability they'd managed to build. She hated the fact that she was going to have to be the one to crush Maxim's hopes that his wife might be okay, to be the one to send him down into the depths of grief.

The interior of the library was peaceful and modern, the ground floor looking like it had been remodeled in the last couple of years. There were plenty of small niches and comfortable chairs, with surprisingly few books on display. Maya guessed that they were all on the other levels of the building. A curving reception desk dominated the entryway, and a young woman with dark hair and glasses looked over at Maya and Marco as they approached.

"Hi, I'm Naomi, can I help you?"

Maya flashed her badge. "I'm Agent Gray, with the FBI. This is Agent Spinelli. We're looking for Maxim Hart. We need to speak to him."

"He… this isn't a great time right now. He's in the archive room."

"Where is that?" Maya asked.

Naomi sighed and led the way to a side room, protected by an electronic lock. She opened the door for Maya, and almost as soon as she did so, Maya heard a howl of anguish coming from beyond it. She heard the pure grief there in that cry and knew that she and Marco were too late; Maxim Hart already knew that his wife was dead.

Maya gestured for Marco to stay behind and made her way into the room, where shelf after dusty shelf reached towards the ceiling. There were boxes and files on those shelves, ancient looking books and bound collections of letters, looking far more like what she'd imagined when she'd thought of a university library. Maya hurried through the stacks there and found Maxim Hart curled up in a crouch, hugging himself while he cried. Papers lay scattered across the floor.

"Mr. Hart?" Maya said, in a soft tone. She knelt beside Maxim, reaching out to put a comforting hand on his shoulder.

"She's gone. I heard… on the local news. She's gone."

Maya silently cursed Lisa Franklin then. "Yes," she admitted. "I'm very sorry for your loss."

Maxim Hart looked up at her, his eyes wild. "Have you caught who did this yet?"

"Not yet," Maya replied.

"It's that crazy janitor," Maxim said. "Why haven't you arrested him?"

"What crazy janitor?" Maya asked, her interest suddenly piqued at the possibility of a lead. If there was a suspect out there at whom Maxim could point them, Maya was more than grateful.

"Todd something… Matthews. Todd Matthews. He works here. He was constantly pestering Evelyn, trying to get information from her about cases."

"Why do you say that he's crazy?" Maya asked, wanting more detail.

"You never met him. He's… creepy. Totally obsessed. I find him in the stacks, sometimes, just reading book after book on criminology, historical crimes, that kind of thing. One of the library assistants interrupted him once and he started shouting, aggressive enough that we had to throw him out. The only reason he still has a job here is because his sister's a lawyer, and she steps in every time he does something like that."

"We'll look into him," Maya assured him. "For now, you should probably head home."

"I… yes." Maxim seemed to be in a daze as he stood, and Maya led him back to the door.

"I've got him," Naomi said, leading him away, deeper into the library.

"That wasn't the way we wanted him to find out," Marco said.

Maya shook her head. "No. He did give us one potential lead. Look up a guy called Todd Matthews, and see what you can find out."

"On it," Marco said, taking out his phone.

While he was doing it, Maya used her own phone to start looking through Laura Gibson's social media.

"It looks as if he's some podcaster," Marco said. "He runs a true crime podcast and, get this, there's a whole series of episodes on the Moonlight Killer."

That would have been enough to catch Maya's interest, but as she scrolled through Laura Gibson's social media feed, she found plenty more to hold her attention. Todd Matthews' name was there again and again, asking detailed forensic questions, demanding answers.

Why won't you tell us anything, one comment demanded. *People like you make me sick, sitting in your ivory towers. I bet you wouldn't be this aloof if a serial killer were coming after you or someone you love.*

Maya showed the comment to Marco, who raised an eyebrow. "I think we need to find Todd right now."

CHAPTER ELEVEN

"Todd has a police record," Maya said, as they drove over to Todd Matthews' address. The property was listed as belonging to his sister, Virginia Matthews, and was on the edge of the town.

"What kind of record?" Marco asked, his eyes not wavering from the road ahead.

Maya scanned through the file, trying to get a sense of the man they were going to meet.

"Todd Matthews, 35, multiple arrests for disturbing the peace, one for assault. Never any charges pressed. I get the impression that he has some kind of mental health issues. He was found one time, standing in the middle of a public fountain, shouting about how he knew exactly who Jack the Ripper was."

"The kind of guy who seems harmless, right up to the point when he isn't," Marco said. "The house should be just down here."

They were out in Miltonberg's suburbs, where the houses sat in near identical rows. There were the almost obligatory minivans on the driveways and a few even had white picket fences around their yards. It seemed peaceful, even idyllic. Could a killer really be lurking there?

The house they pulled up outside could have been any of the others, with nothing to tell it apart from its neighbors, aside, perhaps, from the battered pickup sitting on the driveway next to a much sleeker and more expensive SUV. The pickup had bags in the back, some filled with leaves and grass cuttings, one looking like it was for tools.

Maya got out of the car and marched up to the door with Marco alongside her. Maya wasn't sure what to expect. Would Todd try to fight, to bluff? Would he simply answer all of their questions and explain everything?

As Maya approached the door, she saw a man coming around the side of the building. He was in his thirties, with messy, dark hair and glasses. He was tall and gangly, wearing shorts, sneakers and a white t-shirt. He was instantly familiar from the picture on his police fire.

"Todd Matthews?" Maya said. She pulled out her ID. "I'm Agent Gray, with the FBI. This is Agent Spinelli."

She didn't even get to the end of the sentence before Todd Matthews turned and started to run.

"Todd, stop!" Maya called after him, as she and Marco set off after him. Maya ran with all the speed she could get from her legs, her arms pumping, her heart beating faster as the adrenaline of the chase flooded through her.

Todd burst through a small side gate, heading into the yard of the house. Todd was already rushing towards the back of the yard and the fence that stood there. He flung himself at that fence, leaping over it with the speed and athleticism of a desperate man.

Maya didn't slow down even for a second. She'd scaled much higher obstacles in her FBI and military training. She clambered over the fence as quickly as she could, rolling over the top and hitting the ground running again. Todd was ahead, running down a side path that looked as if it led back towards the front of the house.

Maya realized that he was trying to get to his truck. Maybe he had a weapon there, or maybe he just hoped that if he made it to the vehicle, he might be able to finally get away. Maya couldn't let him do that. Gritting her teeth, she put on another burst of speed.

Marco wasn't with her anymore. Clearly, the fence had slowed him down, or he'd decided to go another way. That meant that it was down to Maya to take Todd down. She couldn't let him get away, because then he would be free to keep killing. Maya couldn't risk the lives of other women around the university. She had to stop him.

Maya was closing on Todd now, as they reached the front of the house again. Sure enough, Todd was going for his truck. He glanced back and seemed to realize that Maya was too close, that he would never be able to pull away before she dragged him from the driver's seat and arrested him. Instead, he went for the flatbed, and the bags sitting there. Maya reached for her gun, not knowing what Todd was going to come out with. She stood there, the weapon levelled at him, as Todd whirled with a wrench in his hand.

Maya had a moment to decide what she was going to do. Todd obviously intended to use the wrench as a weapon, but it wasn't as dangerous as if he'd been holding a knife or a gun. If he rushed Maya, she might have to fire, but she didn't want to, not then. She needed answers.

Todd moved forward, and Maya started to suspect that she might not have a choice. Thankfully, that was when Marco hit him from the side with a tackle that sent both of them sprawling to the ground. The wrench went spinning away, and Marco came up on top, holding Todd down. Maya covered him with her Glock.

"Lie still, Todd. Give it up."

It should have been an easy arrest then. Marco could cuff him and they could take him to the local PD to question him. Yet, even as Maya got ready to read Todd his rights, a woman came bursting out of the house.

Maya could see the similarities between her and Todd at once. She was tall and dark haired, with angular features. She was wearing dark slacks and a cream blouse, while her shoes were designer. She looked absolutely furious, and Maya had to take a second to make sure that she wasn't armed.

"Let go of my brother this *instant*!" she shouted, moving forward.

"Stay where you are, ma'am," Maya instructed.

"The hell I will. You're on my property, and you're assaulting my brother. You'd better identify yourselves at once."

"I'm Agent Gray, with the FBI," Maya said. "This is my partner, Agent Spinelli. We came here to question your brother in connection with the deaths of Laura Gibson and Evelyn Hart."

"Dr. Hart is dead too?" Todd said, from where Marco was holding him down. He sounded surprised. Was that genuine, or just something he was faking?

"That still doesn't explain why you're assaulting him," the woman who had to be Virginia said.

"He ran the moment we identified ourselves," Maya said. "Why did you do that, Todd?"

Virginia answered before Todd could say anything. "My brother has had a number of run ins with the local police, as I'm sure you know. His mental state is often very… fragile. These days, he tends to assume that *any* law enforcement official he sees is there to hurt him or arrest him unless proven otherwise. Now, let my brother *up*, or I'll be making a formal complaint to your superiors."

Maya looked over to Marco and nodded. Marco pulled Todd to his feet, but still kept one hand on his arm, ready in case he tried to run again.

"We still have questions," Maya said.

"What kind of questions?" Virginia shot back.

Maya turned to Todd. "Todd, did you know Laura Gibson and Evelyn Hart?"

Todd nodded. "They work at the university. I've tried to get them on my podcast. Wait, you're *Maya* Gray? And you're Marco Spinelli?"

Maya nodded. It seemed strange that Todd's main reaction to being taken down was this. She was starting to see just how odd he was. She saw Virginia frown.

"You know these agents, Todd?"

Todd smiled then. "They're the ones who took down the Moonlight Killer. And now people think he's back, so they're here. Because Dr. Gibson and Dr. Hart teach about the Moonlight Killer."

That was enough to make Maya pause. "What do you mean, they 'teach about the Moonlight Killer'?"

"They use him as a case study in their courses," Todd said.

That was enough to make Maya pause. It seemed that this case had yet another Moonlight Killer connection that she hadn't known about.

Todd kept going. "It was why I wanted to talk to them. Only he isn't back, is he? The details aren't right."

Maya shook her head. "So we have to look for another killer. One with a connection to both of the professors. One who had access to the campus and who would know which security cameras were broken."

"You seriously believe that my brother would hurt anybody?" Virginia demanded, sounding affronted.

"He's been arrested for assault before," Marco pointed out. "And he was quick to threaten us."

"It doesn't make him a killer," Virginia said. "And that was all a misunderstanding. Sometimes, the world gets too much for him, and he can lash out if people try to force him to do something he doesn't want to. There's a big step between that and premeditated murder."

"You like the Moonlight Killer though, don't you, Todd?" Maya asked.

"He's an important serial killer to study," Todd said, in the enthusiastic tone of someone who had hit upon a subject he loved. "To kill people like that without any obvious reason… to leave no evidence like that… it's very impressive."

"But evil, Todd," Virginia pointed out.

Todd appeared to think for a moment. "Yes, obviously. But that doesn't stop it being impressive. Especially when he was able to kidnap all those women and make the whole FBI do what he wanted."

"One of those women was my sister, Todd," Maya said.

"I know," Todd said. He frowned as if trying to work out why Maya had pointed that out. "Do you think she would want to be on my podcast?"

"No," Maya said, firmly. "I don't."

Maya heard Virginia sigh. "Todd isn't very good at reading social cues. So, let's clear this up. You believe that he is a suspect, yes?"

Maya nodded.

"Well, I can tell you that, for the night of Laura Gibson's murder, he was here, at home, with me."

"I was livestreaming," Todd said.

"When did the other professor die?" Virginia asked.

"Earlier today," Maya said.

"I was home today," Todd said. "Working on my podcast. I want to do a special episode about Dr. Gibson."

"And I can confirm that," Virginia said. "Because I have been working from home today. Todd has not left the house or the yard. His truck has been in the driveway all day, and he was in my view while he was gardening, so there is no way he could have slipped away."

It was a good alibi, and enough to make disappointment flood through Maya. Yes, there was a chance that the sister might be trying to cover for her brother, especially when it seemed that she'd spent so much time looking after him. But Maya didn't get the feeling that Virginia was lying, and Todd… well, he came across more as odd than as dangerous.

Maya looked over to Marco, seeing the disappointment mirrored on his face.

"Thank you for your time," he said, letting go of Todd. "If you think of anything that might be relevant to this case, please get in contact with us."

He handed over a card to Virginia.

"I think that is highly unlikely," Virginia replied.

Maya and Marco headed back to their car.

"It's possible that the alibi is fake," Marco said.

"Maybe, but I don't think so. There will be too many neighbors who will be able to confirm that Todd was gardening, and that his truck at least has been here all day," Maya said.

"So, we're back to square one?"

"Todd did tell us one interesting thing," Maya pointed out. "Did you catch it? Both of the professors used the Moonlight Killer as a case study. The more this case goes on, the more links to him there seem to be."

CHAPTER TWELVE

"If it's not Hanratty, do you think it might be one of his followers?" Marco asked, across the table they were sharing. "We know now that he has people who are willing to do what he asks."

Maya picked at her food, a plate of fries with a side salad. "I'm not sure. I'd have thought… we know he doesn't like people copying his methods. Look at the ones he killed after I solved the cases they were involved in."

There had been several killers who had seemed to try to disguise their work as that of the Moonlight Killer. In at least a couple of cases, after Maya had exposed the truth, they had been found dead. Maya couldn't imagine someone who was that jealous of his methods allowing his followers to copy him the way this killer seemed to be.

"It must mean something that both victims were doing research on the Moonlight Killer, though," Marco said.

Maya thought so, too, but it was hard to see exactly *how* it was relevant.

"There are all kinds of ways that might fit in," she said. "Yes, maybe it could be Hanratty or one of his followers, eliminating people who… what? Aren't doing them justice somehow? No, I don't believe that. Besides, they would have to kill a lot more people all around the country if that were true."

"Maybe we're looking at someone working in the same field, then," Marco suggested. "Or some obsessive fan of the Moonlight Killer, or someone who thinks that people shouldn't do that kind of research, shouldn't glorify a serial killer."

"Is that how you see it?" Maya asked. She thought about the book she'd started writing in the period before Hanratty's escape, the one in which she'd set out to tell her side of the story of catching the Moonlight Killer.

"I don't know," Marco said. "All of these books, podcasts, articles… some of them are obviously trying to understand why and how killers commit their crimes. Some feel as though they're just exploiting the dead."

"Like mine?" Maya asked.

"At least it was your story to tell," Marco replied, although Maya knew that he'd never been entirely comfortable with the book Maya had been writing.

Nor had her sister, Megan. She'd viewed it as Maya getting obsessed, getting pulled back into something that Megan wanted to put behind herself. Maya wondered if there might be someone out there who felt just as strongly and who might be trying to stop those they saw as exploiting their story for personal gain.

Maya had been writing partly as a way to make sense of what had happened, partly as a way to keep looking into the Moonlight Killer's cases.

Thoughts of Megan made Maya take out her phone.

"I need to make a call," she said to Marco. She punched in Megan's number and it wasn't long before her sister picked up, sounding bright and happy.

"Hey, Maya."

Did Maya have a right to intrude on that happiness with her fears? Maya decided that she did, if it meant keeping her sister safe.

"Megan, is everything okay out there?"

"Why wouldn't it be?"

"You haven't noticed anything strange? Anyone lurking around?"

There was a pause. "You're scaring me, Maya. Is this another attempt to get me to take protective custody?"

If Maya thought that Megan would accept it, then she would push that again in a heartbeat. As it was, she knew that she would need to think of another way to protect Megan.

"No, but I'd feel a lot happier if you weren't at home for a few days."

"Why, Maya? What's made you suddenly call with this?"

Maya wasn't sure how much she could tell her sister. On one hand, Megan had suffered at the hands of the Moonlight Killer, along with his other kidnapping victims. She knew exactly how dangerous he was, and she deserved as much of the truth as Maya could give her. On the other, she was still a civilian, and Maya wasn't meant to hand out details of an active investigation.

Maya made a decision. She had to persuade Megan, had to let her know just how serious this was.

"The case I'm working on at the moment has signs of a connection to the Moonlight Killer," Maya said. "Not Hanratty himself, the M.O.

isn't quite right, but it's close. Someone is killing people who are connected to the Moonlight Killer case. Combine that with Hanratty's escape, and… it might be better if you stayed with a friend."

Megan didn't say anything. Maya got the feeling that she was trying to make a decision.

"You're asking me to disrupt my whole life when it might be nothing," she said.

"And if it's something?" Maya countered. "I'm not asking you to go into witness protection. I'm not asking you to give up your whole life. Just… don't be where you normally are. Don't follow your usual schedule."

"I guess… I guess I could go stay with some people for a couple of days. But I'm not doing it long term, Maya."

"Thank you," Maya said. "Just give me a chance to make sure that everything is safe."

She hoped that she would be able to do that. She hoped that, once this case was wrapped up and once Swift's team had put Hanratty back in prison again, things would be safe. She just hoped that those things would happen quickly because everyone connected with the case was in danger until then.

"I love you, sis," Maya said, and hung up.

"You know that Megan probably isn't in danger from this?" Marco said.

"Probably isn't enough," Maya retorted. "And we still need to find answers. We also need to identify who else is in danger."

"You're thinking that there might be more professors out there using the Moonlight Killer as an example in their courses?" Marco said.

Maya was all but certain of it. "This is a town where one of his kills took place, and there are plenty of fields besides forensics and criminal psychology where it might be a useful case study. The odds are that other professors will have used the case simply because it's relevant now that Hanratty has been brought in."

Which would mean they were in danger.

"So, how do we go about finding out who used that kind of thing in their courses?" Marco asked. "The course handbooks won't detail every case study used in a given subject."

No, which meant that they would have to find another way to get answers.

“We need to contact the university administration,” Maya said. "If we get them to send out a warning to their staff, maybe anyone with a connection to the Moonlight Killer through their courses will contact us. We can also get them to send us any information that they think might be relevant.”

“It might work,” Marco said. “But what if someone doesn’t read the message? What if they don’t take it seriously?”

“We just have to hope that, with two people dead, they have every reason to take it very seriously indeed.”

CHAPTER THIRTEEN

"What I'm saying, Nicholas, is that your profile doesn't quite work," Prof. Aaron Sullivan said.

"But I put all weekend into it," his student complained, from the other side of the computer screen. Tutorials had gotten a lot simpler since video conferencing software improved.

"Time doesn't matter," Prof. Sullivan said. "The details do. You can't just say 'the Moonlight Killer was crazy'."

"I point out that his crimes were probably the result of an anti-social personality disorder," his student complained.

"Which amounts to the same thing," Aaron said. "You should be bringing in other strands for your paper. A criminologist doesn't get to come up with such a simple answer. There were the signs of early abuse, the dead parents, the time in the military. There was the question of how he had gone undetected for so long. There was the more intriguing question of how he had always seemed to find people willing to help him. Was that down to some strange charisma, some method of manipulation he'd learned in the special forces, or something else?"

Aaron was going on too long, especially since those were all things that he planned to cover in his own book on the subject.

"Should I put in a section the secret military unit he was supposedly a part of."

Aaron shook his head. "Not unless you have the clearance to get the details, Nicholas."

Which he didn't, and nor did Aaron. It made the quest for the truth more frustrating.

"Go back and do it again," Aaron said. "Give me it by Monday at the latest."

He heard Nicholas sigh, but he didn't care. Sometimes, people had to learn the hard way. He ended the video call then stood, working out some of the kinks in his back, stretching out his lean frame and running a hand through his short, blond hair.

Aaron enjoyed working from home. It meant that he could have all the comforts of his small house near the university campus. It meant that he had his own coffeemaker, his comfortable chair, his cats.

It meant that he didn't have to put up with students in person.

That was harsh. It wasn't as if Aaron was one of those professors who despised the very existence of students, not like some other professors he could think of. It was just that the students seemed to think that the university experience was *all* about them.

When he was in his office on the campus, they were always dropping by, with no respect for office hours, often with problems they could have solved themselves if they'd only taken the time to do the reading properly. They interrupted him in the library, they wanted more time for papers or advice on what they should read next. If Aaron gave in to every demand for his time, he would never get anything else done.

That would be a problem, since Aaron had research papers and textbooks to write. That was the job: to research and try to find new knowledge in the world. Publish or perish. Teaching that knowledge to a bunch of kids who all thought that they were going to be running the FBI one day wasn't an afterthought, exactly, but it *was* secondary.

Which made those days when Aaron could simply sit at home writing all the more precious. He stared at the screen, trying to gauge his progress. The second section of the article was still giving him problems. It needed some key detail to hang the argument on, some fresh angle that might make it come to life.

Aaron heard a crash from downstairs, followed by the mewling of his cats. He sighed; it seemed that he was destined never to get any peace, even in his own home.

"Stop fighting you two. I know. I *know* it's time to feed you. I'm coming."

Aaron headed downstairs into the kitchen, where he saw that the cats had managed to knock over an ornament from the countertop, a piece with the Moonlight Killer's tattoo logo on it. Aaron cursed, because he'd been planning on taking that to an academic conference as a way of catching attention. Now, it lay in a half dozen pieces.

"Damn it, Smudge, Jasper!" Aaron called out. "You couldn't find something else to push off the worktop?"

He guessed that this was his own fault. He should have known better than to leave anything he wanted in one piece where the cats could get at it. Getting out a dustpan and brush, he swept up the pieces, then put down fresh kibble for the two cats. Maybe that would keep them from causing trouble for a while. Long enough for him to finish his work today, at least.

With the cats fed, Aaron decided to take a break long enough to feed himself as well. Coffee to start with, espresso to try to give him the energy to finish the work. As for food… well, he'd never really moved on from student tastes as much as he might have wanted to. He settled for grabbing some ramen, bulking it out with some beef strips, quickly fried. The garbage needed to be taken out, so Aaron carried it outside. He was surprised to find that the back door to the house was unlocked. Had he forgotten to lock it the last time he'd been out that way? If so, that was careless. He knew better than anyone all the ways that crime could sneak into ordinary places.

If not…

Briefly, Aaron felt a rush of fear. He grabbed a knife from the kitchen rack and then started to move around the house, checking for any danger. That was probably stupid in itself, because what if he found something? What was he going to do then? He was an academic, not some kind of… knife fighter.

Finally, Aaron felt happy that the house was secure. He went back to the kitchen door, locking it securely, then put his knife back where it belonged, feeling faintly stupid about the whole thing.

He went back upstairs, returning to his computer, trying to recover his train of thought, trying to push aside the nagging sense that something was wrong. He'd proved that the only thing wrong was his own tendency to forget when he had and hadn't locked the door.

Aaron stretched again, sat down, and stared at the screen, trying to work out what he wanted to write next. There had to be a way to make the whole thing better, to improve it to the point where an academic journal would take it. Aaron just couldn't see it yet.

A notification pinged on his screen, informing him that there was an email from the dean of the university. Aaron sighed and opened it, because as much as an email like this promised academic red tape, Aaron knew he had to deal with it. What would it be? A student who had been caught plagiarizing? Someone making a claim for additional time on an essay? Some problem with the latest batch of academic feedback forms?

Dear Colleagues, the email read, *if you're receiving this, it's because you're in an academic area that might conceivably be relevant to the events taking place around campus at the moment. Following the deaths of two of our colleagues, the FBI have asked me to send this email, asking anyone whose studies touch upon the so called Moonlight Killer to contact me by replying to this email.*

In addition, they have asked that anyone with any information about Evelyn Hart or Laura Gibson, in particular regarding any connections between them or people who might wish them harm, reply in the same way.

Dean Hargreaves

Aaron read through the email twice, mostly to make sure that it wasn't some kind of strange joke, but it seemed to be absolutely in earnest. It occurred to him that he was exactly the kind of person who should probably reply to the email, so he opened up a draft, trying to work out what to write.

Aaron was still staring at the screen when he heard the sound of a footstep behind him. He started to turn, but he was too slow. Something went around his neck, bright and sharp, and that was the last thing he knew before darkness claimed him.

CHAPTER FOURTEEN

"It's getting late," Marco said. "We should head back and start fresh in the morning."

Maya didn't want to stop now, though, not when there was still so much to chase down. They had to get the final word from the coroner on Evelyn Hart, for one thing, just in case there was anything different about this crime scene that might point them towards the killer. There were forensic reports starting to come in, and the witness statements from the people in the park. Each one demanded her and Marco's attention.

"Just a little longer," Maya said. She and Marco were ensconced in a spare office of the Miltonberg PD, which looked as if it was mostly used for storing boxes, with a desk crammed in between and a small window that showed the darkening sky. "If there's something, anything in all these reports, we need to find it."

The local cops seemed to be leaving them alone unless they asked for something specific. Probably they thought that this wasn't their case, so why should they do anything on it? That suited Maya; it meant that Marco and she were free to investigate as they wished.

"I'm not sure that we're making that much progress just going through the files," Marco said.

Maya could only agree with that; so far, there wasn't any new information for them to work with. Nothing that might point to exactly why this was happening, or who might have done it.

"Have you found any more connections between the two victims?" Maya said.

Marco shrugged. "As far as I can tell, the problem is that there are too *many* connections. They're women of a similar age, both working in crime related fields, they're on several interdisciplinary working groups, they've even presented at the same conferences. And, of course, there's the Moonlight Killer connection."

That was the big one, the one that it was impossible to ignore. It couldn't be a coincidence that both Laura and Evelyn had been working on things connected to the Moonlight Killer cases. Maya just wasn't sure what the connection was. Was it someone obsessed with Hanratty? Some shared student? Some colleague of theirs?

Maya tried to concentrate on the possibilities, but by this point, they were starting to swim in her head.

"Maya, we're both exhausted," Marco said. "Let's not even head home. We'll grab a place to stay here and start first thing in the morning. Maybe if we come at this fresh, we'll be able to see something that we're missing now."

"Okay," Maya said, giving in at last. She knew that Marco was right; staring at the evidence now wasn't going to get them any further. She got up, grabbing her jacket and heading for the door.

She'd almost reached it when Officer Bryant came rushing in. "Agents, you'd better come quickly."

"What is it, Bryant?" Maya asked.

"There's been another murder!"

***

The house wasn't far from the university's campus. It was small compared to the houses near it, sitting in the middle of a neat, flower-trimmed lawn with a curved driveway at the front. An old sedan sat on that driveway, presumably belonging to the victim.

Maya was frustrated and angry as she and Marco drove towards it. Frustrated that they hadn't been able to make more progress. Angry that it had cost someone else their life. It seemed that, no matter how hard they pushed on this case, they weren't getting anywhere, and another innocent person had paid the price.

By the time Maya and Marco reached the house, there were already several police cruisers near it, lights flashing in the darkness as they sought to contain the scene. Maya could see uniformed officers rushing about, some closing off the house, others working to question everyone nearby.

There was quite a crowd there, standing around as if waiting for news of whatever had happened inside. Most of them looked like a collection of neighbors and friends from the surrounding houses. There was one face, though, that Maya recognized instantly.

"Agents!" Lisa Franklin called out as soon as Maya and Marco left their car. The reporter had her phone out as usual, training the camera on them. "Two murders in one day! Does this mean that the killer is accelerating their timetable? Are they doing it because they know that the FBI are here?"

"We don't have any details yet," Maya said, heading towards the house.

"Are you even making any progress on this case?" Lisa demanded, her tone suddenly acerbic. "Shouldn't it bother you that a killer is somehow getting away with murdering innocent people? Are you going to admit to my readers that they're proving too clever for you?"

Maya felt a wave of anger and the sudden urge to snap back at the reporter, but she knew that was what Lisa probably wanted. She wanted a reaction that she could show to the world. Instead, Maya moved forward, ignoring her.

"She's here quickly again," Marco murmured to Maya as they left the reporter behind.

Maya nodded. So far, it seemed that Lisa Franklin was everywhere they looked. Maya did her best to ignore the reporter. She knew that she couldn't let her get under her skin.

Maya walked around the perimeter of the house, wanting to see that much before she went inside. Everything was pristine and quiet. A couple of cats peered at her from the bushes in the yard, shying away from the noise and lights out front. Maya went around to the back door. It proved to be open, and she doubted that the police would have unlocked it. Was this how the killer had gained access? She took pictures of the lock, looking for any telltale marks that might indicate that it had been drilled or picked.

Opening it carefully, she went inside. There were already police and forensic investigators swarming the house, looking for any evidence. The house was small and filled with oddities on shelves: a pair of handcuffs, a police truncheon that looked a century old at least. The kinds of things that someone obsessed with the police might keep. There were photographs of police from different countries in different times. There was even one of J. Edgar Hoover, the founder of the FBI.

Bryant was in there now, talking to a couple of other cops. He broke away and came over to Maya.

"What do we have?" Maya asked.

"It looks like the victim is Aaron Sullivan, thirty-five years old, another professor at the university."

Which made three, the link impossible to ignore. But this victim was male, which represented a difference in approach from the killer. Could that detail prove to be important?

"What's his specialty?" Maya asked.

"Criminology."

Another subject where he might reasonably use the Moonlight Killer as a case study. Another victim who might reasonably have known the others and met them professionally. Again, it felt as if the problem wasn't finding links, it was that there were too many.

"The back door is unlocked," Maya said. "How did the first cops on the scene get in?"

"Through the front," Bryant said. "It had been left hanging open, with the lights off in the house. A neighbor called us, and the first unit on the scene found the body."

"Where is he?" Marco asked.

Bryant jerked his head upwards. "Upstairs."

Maya headed for the stairs. She could feel a familiar sense of dread rising within her, although it wasn't the same as when she'd been approaching the spot where Evelyn Hart died earlier. There, Maya hadn't known if the professor was alive or dead. Now, she knew for certain that the worst had happened.

The smell of death hit her as she reached the top of the stairs, mingled with the iron tang of blood. Maya could have guessed which room the body was in just from that, but the presence of the coroner's team made it even more obvious.

Maya pushed open the door to what proved to be a study lined with bookshelves. Those shelves contained works on criminology and psychology, the history of crime and related works. None of that mattered, not compared to the scene at one side of the room. ,

A blond haired, blue eyed man sat on a chair, several feet from the desk on which his computer sat. It looked to Maya as if he'd been dragged backwards, and the wire garotte around his throat said how. Maya winced at the sight, and at the blood that lay between that spot and the desk.

"If the killer ambushed him from behind and dragged him back," Marco said. "Wouldn't the chair have fallen over?"

Maya nodded. That made sense. "Which means that the killer put everything back to pose him like this. Just as with the others. It also explains the open door. The killer wanted us to find him."

It was in stark contrast to the way the Moonlight Killer had worked, ambushing his victims and abandoning them where they fell, not caring if anyone found them or not.

“So, he wants notoriety from this?” Marco asked, starting to move around the room, obviously looking for any traces of evidence.

Maya went to the computer, managing to open it with just a quick keypress. “That, or he wants us to see that he’s killed his victim for some other reason. To show us that they’re being punished, perhaps?”

Maya looked on the screen, and wasn’t entirely surprised to find a research paper on the Moonlight Killer there waiting. It was good to have the link confirmed, but she wasn’t sure what to do with it.

“There’s nothing obvious here,” Maya said, starting to back out of the room, grateful that she could leave the scene there behind. Maya had seen the dead far too many times by now, but that still didn’t make it easy.

“So, where do you want to start with this?” Marco asked.

Maya sighed. There was going to be a lot to do tonight. “We’ll need to talk to the neighbors in case anyone saw anything. I want to sweep the wider area for footprints, and check if Prof. Sullivan knew the other victims well. But I’m also wondering, if this is all connected to the fact that they all use the Moonlight Killer as a case study, how the killer knows that.”

“We’re looking for someone with access to their curricula?” Marco asked. “Maybe a student?”

“That’s what I’m wondering,” Maya said. “We need to look for any students the three have in common, then start to go through them to see if any of them has a worrying obsession with the Moonlight Killer.”

It was going to be a long night. Maya only hoped that it would let them find the killer before they struck again.

CHAPTER FIFTEEN

Maya was back in the bunker, trying to free her sister, trying to get to Megan before it was too late.

She moved carefully, stepping over the traps that Francis Hanratty had put in place. She knew how much he loved to leave traps. Her rifle swung left and right, covering the angles. She had to do this alone, because there was no one else she could trust to do this.

Maya knew that this was a dream, but somehow that didn't stop the feeling of fear that filled her, the certainty that something was wrong. The bunker seemed to stretch and twist with that fear, the route turning into something mazelike.

And this time, it seemed, Hanratty wasn't alone. Figures came at Maya out of the dark tunnels of the bunker, dressed in black, faceless. Maya fired, the rifle booming in the confines of the tunnels, bringing one down, then another. Yet somehow, there were always more.

They charged in, and now Maya was fighting hand to hand, struggling to keep them all at bay. They overwhelmed her, pinning her down, taking her weapon, and now Hanratty was there. He had Megan in his arms, and now the strangling rope was around her neck…

Maya woke with a start, sunlight hurting her eyes. Marco was shaking her shoulder, holding out coffee with the other hand. In that moment, he had never looked as good. Maya took the coffee gratefully, gulping it down, feeling the caffeine hit her system.

"How long was I asleep?" she asked.

"Not long," Marco said. "Probably not long enough. You need some proper rest, Maya."

"I'll get real sleep when whoever's doing this is behind bars," Maya said.

She looked at the piles of papers in front of her. Most seemed to be witness statements from the people around Aaron Sullivan's house. Maya hadn't been able to find anything in them so far.

"The list of students taking the three professors' courses has come through at last," Marco said.

"That's good," Maya replied. "Maybe there's a connection there. We need to start going through it, checking each student on the list."

"That could take a while," Marco replied.

He put a sheet of paper down on the desk. There had to be thirty names on it at least. Maya cursed to herself. She should have guessed that there would be plenty of students who took all three classes. Criminology, forensics, and criminal psychology had too many natural overlaps for it to be any other way.

Thirty students to look at. Thirty students where Maya and Marco would need to look at their police records, their social media accounts, where they would need to talk to their supervisors to see if any of them stood out as behaving oddly or showing too much interest in the professors.

"The university also sent over access to the three professors' university email and messaging accounts," Marco said. "That should allow us to see if anyone was making threats against them."

Maya guessed that she should feel grateful for so much information at her fingertips. Instead, it felt almost overwhelming, even for her.

"You start looking through the messages," Maya said. "I'll start working my way through the list of students."

It was slow going. The first student on the list, Rachel Adams, didn't have any kind of criminal record, but Maya guessed that would be true of most of them. She couldn't rely on that as the only potential red flag. Instead, she started to look through the student's social media accounts, looking for any sign of an unhealthy obsession with the Moonlight Killer in particular.

Maya moved on to the next name on the list, repeating the process. She still hadn't called any of the students' supervisors. She figured that it was better to leave that until the end of the process, when maybe she would have narrowed the list of names down to something more manageable. She also suspected that college supervisors wouldn't be in a hurry to report any of their students as behaving strangely to the FBI.

It was still incredibly slow going, because Maya was looking for small details, a picture or a post that might point to some kind of link to the Moonlight Killer, maybe something from around the time of the first murder in the town, the one for which Hanratty had been convicted.

Maya rubbed her eyes, looking away from the list for a moment or two. She took a moment to check her email, remembering the request that she and Marco had had the university authorities put out. She wasn't particularly hopeful that she would get much, but if she could at least identify lecturers who had done work on the Moonlight Killer, she might know who the killer might try to target next.

Maya was quite surprised to find a very different email in her inbox, sent from what appeared to be an anonymous address. Apparently, someone didn't want the FBI to identify them. Maya suspected that the FBI's techs might be able to grab the IP address that the email had been sent from, but in a university, that might not be very helpful.

Hi,

I just received the dean's email asking us to contact you if we'd seen anything suspicious. I don't really want to get involved, but I can't just not say anything. There's another professor who argued publicly with both Prof. Gibson and Prof. Hart. Prof. Henry Carlson. He hated them.

The email was unsigned, which made Maya wonder whether this was just someone trying to settle a grudge by reporting a colleague or rival to the FBI. Still, with something like this, she couldn't ignore it.

"Marco, we've had a tip. There's a professor called Henry Carlson who supposedly had a grudge against our first two victims. Can you check to see if he appears in any of their messages?"

"I'm on it," Marco said.

While he worked, Maya started to look into Prof. Henry Carlson. He didn't have a police record beyond a couple of unpaid parking tickets. He *did* have a social media channel, where he put up videos of popular history, mostly relating to crime and punishment. It seemed that he also used it as a platform on which to tear down anyone he saw as a rival.

"Why Lauren Gibson's position on blood spatter is stupid," Maya read out. "Why Prof. Gibson is WRONG!" There were a couple more like that, including one entitled "Prof. Hart's theory of the criminal mind, and why it doesn't matter."

This wasn't what she expected from academic debate. This was Carlson engaging in personal attacks in the most public forum possible.

"I found something," Marcus said. "There are some emails here going back and forth between Laura Gibson and Henry Carlson, the two of them arguing about some video he put up. It's… pretty heated."

"Heated enough to kill someone over?" Maya asked.

Marco hesitated. "I'm… not sure. Would someone really kill someone over an academic rivalry?"

"Maybe," Maya said. "This already looks like it's gone beyond the usual limits of an academic argument. Maybe it went *too* far, and now Prof. Carlson has decided to end the argument, permanently."

CHAPTER SIXTEEN

Maya tried to focus on the case during the drive over to the university, but she found her attention drifting to Marco. She'd forgotten what it could be like, working a case with him, him just being there, beside her.

"Do you think the bureau will keep us working cases together when this is done?" Maya asked.

"I'm… not sure," Marco replied. "I guess as long as we're on Swift's team, but after that… they split us up once."

"Would you *like* to keep working together?" Maya asked. She was suddenly nervous. What if Marco said no? He was only here, after all, because Swift had pretty much forced him to be. She'd pulled him from undercover work just to do this. Would Marco resent Maya for that? He'd been gone a lot in the last few months.

Marco looked over at her, and Maya could see the affection, the love, there in his eyes.

"Maya, there is *no one* I would rather be alongside for this."

"But you've been working undercover," Maya pointed out.

"I go where the Bureau sends me," Marco replied. "And I thought before that having some space while we worked might be good for us. But the last case we worked showed me better than that."

The last time they'd worked together, they'd been hunting a serial killer who stalked women from port to port up the East Coast. It had shown how well the two of them worked together, both professionally and personally.

"But if you've wanted to work with me since then," Maya said, "why go back to undercover work? Why leave me to go back to the field office? I thought… I thought you didn't want to be around me."

Marco looked briefly surprised. "Maya, that will *never* be true. But it was never going to be as easy as simply deciding that I wanted to work with you, not when we both had assignments."

"So, I guess we have a lot to thank Agent Swift for, then," Maya said. She really hoped that she would never have to actually admit that to the deputy director.

“We’re here,” Marco said, as they pulled up at the university. “Now, we just have to find Prof. Henry Carlson.”

They headed over to an ivy-covered building that proclaimed itself to be the faculty of history. The interior looked as if it hadn't changed in at least fifty years. Students were making their way along its corridors, while a young woman with short blonde hair sat behind a reception desk, reading a book on the Industrial Revolution.

“We’re looking for Prof. Carlson,” Marco said.

“Office 27b,” the receptionist said, without looking up from her book. “But you won’t want to interrupt him in the middle of a seminar. He tends to shout.”

“We’ll take the risk,” Maya said, heading past her. She and Marco went down the halls of the history faculty, looking for the office they wanted, moving quickly. Office 27b was one of a line of identical doors along a long corridor. Even as Maya approached it, she heard shouting from the other side.

“What is this meant to be? What do you think you’re doing, Garth? There are days when I could just *kill* you, you idiot!”

Maya glanced over at Marco, suddenly wary. Her hand found the grip of her Glock automatically. She knocked once, then opened the door without waiting for an answer.

The interior of the office held an old oak desk, a large leather chair, a couple of much less comfortable looking chairs nearby. There were shelves around the room, some with books, others with ornaments. A skull sat on one of them, a mortarboard hat on top of it.

There were two men in the room. One was a nervous looking young man of perhaps twenty, overweight, with shoulder length dark hair. The other was in his thirties, tall and lanky, with a thinning hairline and rounded features. He was wearing an expensive suit and gesticulating wildly. He didn’t seem to be armed, though. He looked around as Maya and Marco stepped into the room.

“What do you think you’re doing, coming in here uninvited?” he snarled, then seemed to realize that Maya and Marco weren’t students.

Maya held up her badge. “Prof. Carlson? I’m Agent Gray, with the FBI. This is Agent Spinelli. We need to talk to you.”

“Well, then, you can wait and-”

“*Now*, sir,” Marco said, in a firm tone.

Prof. Carlson stopped short, then looked over to his student. “Get out, Garth. And I expect you to rewrite that chapter by Tuesday.”

The younger man all but ran from the office, shutting the door behind him.

"The FBI?" Prof. Carlson said. "What has the FBI barging into my office, without a warrant? Without so much as an *appointment*?"

"We need to talk to you, Professor," Maya said. "About Laura Gibson and Evelyn Hart. I trust you've heard what happened to them?"

"I did," Prof. Carlson said. "Although I fail to see what it has to do with me."

He moved back to the big leather chair, taking a seat. He didn't seem flustered now by Maya and Marco's presence, just irritated.

"You knew the two professors?" Maya said.

"We were colleagues," Prof. Carlson said. "Our paths would cross at academic conferences and so forth."

"And when you tore them down online?" Maya said.

Prof. Carlson shrugged. "That is simply how the world works these days. It isn't enough to be just an academic. One has to have an online presence, a following."

"Which you gained by attacking your colleagues?" Marco asked, looking surprised. "That doesn't sound very professional."

Prof. Carlson shrugged. "I wouldn't expect the two of you to understand. Does either of you even have a college degree? Let alone an advanced qualification?"

"Why don't you explain it, then?" Maya said. She didn't care about the professor's insults. She *did* care about whether his attitude made it more likely that he might attack his colleges in the real world.

"Academia is a dog-eat-dog world. At the best of times, we exist by destroying one another's pet theories. And that's before you throw in the usual academic backbiting, the need for advancement at the expense of one's fellows. In the current world, it has become worse. Colleges want to save money. If you sit in your little corner of academia, trying to get on, there's a good chance that your whole course gets cut. By building an online following, I made myself harder for the university to get rid of. Fame is the one insulator from the fiscal axe. If I have to be negative in order to achieve that, then so be it."

Maya considered that. "So, it's a world where you benefit from your colleagues' failures? Tell me, how much more secure would your position be if two professors working in similar fields weren't around?"

"There is nothing *similar* about my work to that of those hacks," Prof. Carlson said.

"So, you aren't working on anything to do with the Moonlight Killer?" Marco asked.

"Well, yes, I was considering it. Following the escape, it seems that there might be sufficient interest."

"That might not be a good idea," Maya said, trying to gauge whether Prof. Carlson was a killer, or just an asshole.

"Are you trying to dictate what I do and do not work on?" Prof. Carlson gave her a haughty look. "There's such a thing as academic freedom."

"And three professors have been killed because of the links their work had to the Moonlight Killer," Maya snapped back.

Prof. Carlson cocked his head to one side. "Three?"

"Prof. Aaron Sullivan was murdered last night," Maya supplied.

Prof. Carlson paled visibly, his lip trembling. "Aaron? Someone killed *Aaron*?"

"You knew Prof. Sullivan?" Maya asked.

Prof. Carlson stood suddenly. "Of course I knew him! He and I were students together! And you're insinuating that *I* might have had something to do with his death?"

"And Laura's, and Evelyn's," Marco said. "Where were you three nights ago? Yesterday morning? Yesterday evening after nine?"

"Two nights ago, I was at a dinner party," Prof. Carlson said. "As for the rest… here, or the library, or home. Aaron… *really* Aaron?"

Maya nodded. "I'm sorry. We'll need the names of anyone else who was at the dinner party."

At this point, she was starting to believe the alibi, simply because of the shock of Prof. Carlson's face.

Prof. Carlson grabbed a pen and started scribbling on a sheet of paper. He thrust it at Maya. "Here. Names. Now, get out of my office, please. I need to… I hadn't heard about Aaron."

Maya looked over to Marco and gestured to the door. They left, heading back down the corridor.

"What do you think?" Marco asked. "That alibi could be fake."

"It could be," Maya agreed, "but you saw how he reacted when he heard that Aaron Sullivan was dead. I don't think he knew. I don't think Prof. Carlson is a good guy, but I also don't think that he's *our* guy."

"Okay," Marco said. "But where does that leave us? Wading through the profiles of a bunch of students until we randomly hit paydirt?"

Maya shook her head. "I had a thought about that."

CHAPTER SEVENTEEN

"Agent Gray, Agent Spinelli, so good to see you both again!" Prof. Neiman said, as the two of them entered his office. "To what do I owe the pleasure? If this is about the dean's email… well, the Moonlight Killer isn't really my field. Nothing later than about 1970 for me. It's simpler that way."

What did Maya do when there was too much work to get through alone? It turned out that she outsourced.

"Prof. Nieman," she said, "when we met before, you suggested that a couple of your graduate students might want to help with the work on this case. Were you serious about that?"

The white haired, older professor raised one bushy eyebrow. "Yes, of course. Nicholas and Zia would be grateful for the experience, and if I word it right to the dean, I can probably count it as an extra credit assignment for them both."

Maya sighed with relief. It seemed that she and Marco might have a way through the list of students the lecturers shared after all. It might even work out better since a couple of grad students asking about their fellow undergraduates might get answers quicker than the FBI doing it.

"What we want your students to do is to look at the names of the students on this list and see if anything stands out about them," Maya said. "In particular, do they have an obvious fascination with the Moonlight Killer, any grudges against Laura Gibson, Evelyn Hart or Aaron Sullivan, that kind of thing."

"So, a practical exercise in profiling?" Prof. Nieman said.

"If you want to put it like that, yes," Maya replied.

"I do, I do. I shall have them begin at once."

Maya shook the professor's hand, a wave of gratitude sweeping through her. "Thank you, Professor. Take my card. Give me a call if they find anything."

Maya and Marco left the office, Maya feeling as if a weight had been lifted from her.

"You're sure about this?" Marco asked, looking doubtful.

Maya nodded. “It means that we don’t have to spend the whole day looking at students one by one. That doesn't feel like where we’re going to get answers in this case.”

“I’m pretty sure the FBI doesn’t usually hand its work over to grad students,” Marco pointed out.

“They’re just taking an initial pass at this. A couple of criminology grad students should be capable of looking through other students’ social media for any posts enthusing about how much they love the Moonlight Killer.”

“Plenty of people seem to, these days,” Marco said with a sigh as the two of them walked back out into the open air of the campus. “I still don’t get why people would willingly follow a psychopath like that.”

"Because he's charismatic, and he's clever," Maya said. "Because he knows how to manipulate people, and because people see what they want to, most of the time. There are people who see a serial killer, and they buy into this whole mystique of someone free from the constraints placed on them by society. They compare that to their own lives, where they have bosses and rules, and they think it's special."

“That, or there are just more psychopaths out there than we thought, ready to do what he wants.”

That was another possibility, and Maya wasn’t sure which was more dangerous. If Hanratty got ordinary people to do what he wanted, then that gave him a potentially wide pool of followers. If he was somehow organizing other killers and psychopaths, that gave him a group of very dangerous individuals indeed.

“So, now that we have the grad students whittling down the list of people in the victims’ classes, how do you want to approach this next?” Marco asked.

Maya thought, and for the first time in a day or so, it felt as if she wasn’t buried under a mountain of witness statements and meaningless information.

“I want to look a little closer at the victims,” Maya said. “We know that they had students in common, but who else met all three of them? Who might have been in a position to do this?”

They found a quiet spot on the campus from which to continue their research, out in front of a café, under the shade of a large tree. Maya didn’t want to waste time going back to the Miltonberg PD, not when the campus seemed to be at the heart of the investigation. They grabbed their laptops from the car and started to look deeper into the victims.

It wasn't just a case of finding connections. They already had plenty of those. Maya felt as though they already had the one that mattered, too, in the form of their research into the Moonlight Killer. The question was, who would have known that?

Working that out meant researching the three professors, trying to find out if any of their published works were about the Moonlight Killer, or if they'd spent time talking about him. Maya could see papers from the three on everything from "Trace DNA on fibrous surfaces: a comparison" to "Patterns of pickpocketing in NYC subways". Nothing directly referenced the Moonlight Killer.

Maya tried a general search for the victims' names along with the phrase "Moonlight Killer" and was surprised when hits came up immediately. There was a local newspaper article in which Aaron Sullivan talked about the effects of the Moonlight Killer on the town, an interview with Laura Gibson on the physical evidence of the Moonlight Killer's crimes, and a much longer video interview with Evelyn Hart on the psychology of the killer.

Maya's first instinct on seeing those was to curse her luck, since it meant that the whole reading public of Miltonberg would know that the professors had a connection to the Moonlight Killer. It could potentially make anyone a suspect. Then, she looked at the bylines of the articles and stopped short, frowning at the screen, trying to make sense of it.

"What is it?" Marco asked. "You've found something, haven't you?"

"Maybe," Maya said. "You remember that reporter who was at the crime scenes? Lisa Franklin?"

Marco nodded. "What about her?"

"It looks like she's interviewed all three victims on topics relating to the Moonlight Killer."

Marco paused for a second or two. "That could be nothing. She's a reporter, and in a small town like this, the murder of a resident by a serial killer is going to be big news."

Maya knew that, but even so, she started to look deeper at Lisa Franklin's articles, searching for any relating to the Moonlight Killer.

She wasn't entirely prepared for the avalanche of them that hit her computer screen. It seemed that Lisa had written about him again and again, picking up on every kill or potential kill around the country since the one in the town, offering opinion pieces on his motives and methods, his impact and the chances of him being caught. Maya's eye was particularly caught by one entitled "What it takes to be a serial killer", in which it seemed that Lisa was plotting out exactly what it would take to kill someone in the Moonlight Killer's style.

"She's obsessed," Maya said. "This goes way beyond just a few stories because the murder was a huge event in the town."

"I guess so," Marco said.

"And she keeps showing up at every crime scene, far too quickly."

That seemed to be enough to make Marco pause. "You think that she's killing people for the attention? For the stories?"

"I don't know what to think," Maya said. "With her level of obsession, maybe it turned into something more. Maybe it's about trying to recreate something that she's utterly focused on." She took out Lisa Franklin's card. "Whatever the potential motive, we need to talk to her to find out."

She called Lisa, and the reporter picked up after a few rings.

"Hello?"

"Hello, Lisa?" Maya said. "This is Agent Maya Gray."

"Agent Gray." The friendliness in Lisa's voice seemed to go up a couple of notches. "I wasn't expecting to hear from you."

"You said that if I wanted to talk to you, I should call," Maya said. "Well, my partner and I would like to talk to you. Could you meet us down at the local police department? We're borrowing an office there."

"I can be there in a half hour," Lisa said. "Thank you, Agent Gray. I have so many questions for you."

And Maya would have more than a few for the reporter.

CHAPTER EIGHTEEN

“We’re doing this in an interrogation room?” Lisa Franklin said, as Maya ushered her through into the room they’d borrowed from the local PD for the purpose. Marco was following a step or two behind.

“If that’s okay?” Maya said.

Maya saw Lisa looking the room over, with its Gray walls and its metal table bolted to the floor. Maya half expected her to balk at the prospect of going in there, but instead, she smiled.

"It's perfect. I can write a whole story on my time in an FBI interrogation room with the woman who caught the Moonlight Killer."

Maya looked over to Marco, who shrugged. It seemed that it might be easier to get Lisa talking about the Moonlight Killer than Maya might have thought.

The three of them sat down in the interrogation room and Maya set a digital recorder running. Lisa reached into her bag and did the same.

“Do you mind if I record this? It’s so much easier than trying to keep notes.”

“If you want to, sure,” Maya said.

Lisa got a question out before Maya could ask anything. “Great, so what’s it like, being the woman who took down the perfect serial killer?”

“Is that what you think he is?” Maya asked.

Lisa smiled again. “Now, come on, Agent Gray. I’m the reporter here. I should ask the questions.”

“And I’m the FBI agent,” Maya replied. “In the middle of an investigation. We’re here to ask you questions, Lisa, not answer them.”

Lisa Franklin looked momentarily confused. “Wait, I thought you asked me here so that you could give me an interview. Am I a suspect here? Do I need a lawyer?

“Do you?” Marco asked.

Lisa looked suddenly nervous, running one hand through the blonde bob of her hair and glancing towards the door as if she might get up and leave. If she did, would Maya try to stop her? Maya didn’t want it to get to that stage.

"Lisa," she said. "There are some things that have come up in the investigation that we think you might be able to help us with. You've obviously been following the Moonlight Killer case in this town for a while, and you've talked to all three of the victims."

Maya tried to make it sound as if Lisa were a witness, and maybe she was. It was hard to work out exactly *what* she was right then.

"Well, how about we exchange questions?" Lisa asked. "I get my interview and you get your information. I'll go first. What was it like when you first realized that your sister had been kidnapped?"

Maya considered not answering. She thought about simply telling Lisa that she had to answer her and Marco's questions or she risked being arrested. But the truth was that they didn't have enough yet for anything like that and there was a good chance that Lisa would simply clam up. She had to answer.

"I felt horrified," Maya said. "But also guilty."

"Why guilty?"

"My turn for a question, Lisa. Why do you call the Moonlight Killer the perfect serial killer?"

The reporter looked surprised by the question, as if the answer should have been obvious to anyone.

"Because he *is*. There's something pure about the way he kills, stalking his victims, taking them without even giving them a chance to fight back, all while leaving almost no evidence. Even a prison can't hold him. Now, why did you feel guilty?"

Maya knew that she had to keep giving answers in order to get them, but it still hurt to dredge up these parts of the past.

"Megan and I… we'd drifted apart. I thought she'd gone off travelling, but it turns out that he'd kidnapped her, along with eleven other women. I feel guilty for being so caught up with my work that I wasn't there for her." Maya took a breath, choking back the pain of that memory. "You sound like you admire Francis Hanratty."

"Frank," Lisa said. "Doesn't he prefer everyone to call him Frank?"

"That's what he called himself when we caught him," Maya said. "And you haven't answered me. Do you admire him?"

Lisa sat there for several seconds, apparently considering her answer. Maya glanced over to Marco. He had a concerned look, but that seemed to be directed at Maya, not at the reporter.

"I didn't start out that way," Lisa said. "When he started killing, I figured he was just another killer, worth writing a story about sometime maybe, but not much more than that. Then, when he killed someone in

Miltonberg, I started to get more interested. I had to cover the story, of course, and the more I looked into him, the more fascinating he seemed."

"What made him so fascinating?" Marco asked.

Lisa wagged a finger at him. "My turn, I think. One for you, Agent Spinelli. When did you realize that you were in love with Agent Gray? Was it during the case?"

Marco looked as if he wasn't going to answer. Maya was more intrigued by the choice of question. It wouldn't give Lisa any new information about the Moonlight Killer. It seemed like the kind of question to ask only if she were playing games with Maya and Marco. All her questions so far seemed to have been like that, designed to dig up the most personal memories.

"It crept up on me," Marco said. "I was attracted to Maya from the first case we worked together, but we didn't do anything about it, not then. I think almost losing her to the Moonlight Killer was what finally made me realize that I had to do something."

Maya got her next question in quickly. "How have you been at the crime scenes so quickly, Lisa?"

"Oh, I have a police scanner," Lisa said. "And I've been lucky to be close by. Tell me, Agent Gray, what do you think about the fact that the Moonlight Killer has escaped from prison? Are you afraid that he might come after you?"

Maya wasn't sure that she believed that excuse. Even with a scanner, Lisa was always at the scenes *very* quickly.

"The part that scares me is that he had help doing it," Maya replied. "The idea that this psychopath is able to persuade so many other people to work with him, that they would *choose* to work for a madman, that's the scary part."

"Those are very derogatory terms," Lisa said. "Hasn't it occurred to you that maybe you just don't understand the depths of the Moonlight Killer's genius? His message? Maybe the people who follow him just understand him better than you."

"What's his message, Lisa?" Maya asked. "What do you see in him?"

"It's..." Lisa hesitated, as if struggling to put it into words. "It's about freedom, about power. For him, there's no power greater than taking away a life, doing it right at the point when someone has the greatest potential. It's about taking control, taking those moments when they arrive, rather than wasting them. It's about being who you really are."

"And who are you, Lisa?" Maya asked. "Because you seem pretty obsessed with the Moonlight Killer."

"Well, he's been very good for my career. My articles on him do better than anything else, did you know that?"

"Articles like the ones you did with all three victims?" Marco asked.

"I feel like I'm not getting my questions now," Lisa said. "And it sounds like you're starting to treat me like a suspect again."

Maya shrugged. "If you don't want to be a suspect, then just provide us with an alibi for the times of the three murders. Explain why three people you've interviewed have ended up dead."

"I told you I was nearby when the murders happened," Lisa said. "I already admitted that."

"Maybe you were nearby because you were the one doing the killing," Marco suggested.

Lisa shook her head vehemently. "How could you think that?"

"Maybe because you've already described killing as the ultimate power over someone?" Marco said, his tone hardening. "You're obviously obsessed with the Moonlight Killer, you knew the victims, you don't have an alibi, and you said yourself that the first killing was good for your work as a reporter. Maybe you decided that you needed more stories. Maybe you decided to stop waiting for a serial killer to strike again and became one yourself."

Lisa was still shaking her head. "I think I should go."

"You're not going anywhere until you've finished answering our questions," Marco said.

"In that case, I want a lawyer."

Maya got up, walking out of the interrogation room. Now that Lisa had decided to lawyer up, they couldn't keep questioning her. Marco followed her out, closing the door firmly behind him.

"What do you think?" he asked.

"She's suspicious," Maya said. "Very suspicious. The way she went off when we talked about Hanratty's followers makes me wonder if maybe she might be one of them. But we don't have enough hard evidence yet to connect her to any of the crimes."

"Then we find it," Marco said. "We hold her here and get a warrant to search her place. Maybe there will be something there that will connect her firmly to the deaths."

Maya nodded. She wasn't sure if they could get a warrant, given the little that they had, but if they could, then there might be something there that would prove that Lisa Franklin was the killer they were hunting for.

CHAPTER NINETEEN

"This is the place," Maya said, as they pulled up outside Lisa Franklin's apartment building in the heart of town. The brownstone building rose four stories high, with Lisa Franklin's apartment on the top floor.

Maya tried to assess how easy it would be for Lisa to come and go unseen from the building. She guessed that it would be pretty easy, particularly if her neighbors were used to the idea of their local reporter going out to cover stories at every hour of the day and night.

She had the warrant in her hand. It had been easier to get than she thought it might be. It seemed that, after three deaths, the local judge was eager to do what it took to get a resolution to all of this. Maya just hoped that searching Lisa's apartment would supply one.

She and Marco went inside, where they found the building supervisor, a bald man in his late fifties, with watery blue eyes. The nametag on his work clothes proclaimed that he was Dan. Maya handed over the search warrant.

"We have a warrant to search apartment 4a," she said. "Open it up for us, please."

"I'm not sure that Ms. Franklin would-"

"She is currently being held at the local police department," Marco said. "And you've seen the warrant. The alternative is that we break the door open. I'm sure she'd like that even less, and it would mean more work for you."

The building supervisor grumbled under his breath, but led the way up several flights of stairs, finally fishing a big bunch of keys from his belt as he reached the door to Lisa's apartment. He unlocked it, then stepped back.

"It's all yours," Dan said. He turned and headed back towards the stairs. "Make sure it's locked when you leave."

"Thank you," Maya said. She stepped into the apartment carefully. She could feel her heart beating a little faster, her instincts warning her about the possibility of danger. It took her a second or two to realize why her instincts were screaming at her like that. She was so used to anything connected with the Moonlight Killer being trapped that a part of her expected this whole apartment to be one giant kill zone, laced with explosives.

Instead, it seemed to be a normal, rather cluttered, apartment. The living area had a broad couch on a red and green patterned rug, a TV on the wall and an antique coffee table. A small desk to one side held a computer, and Lisa had been quick enough to hand over the password once it was made clear that the alternative was Maya and Marco taking it for the techs at the FBI to crack.

"Check the computer," Maya said. "I'll start to look over the rest of this place."

There were books and papers everywhere, and it took Maya a moment to realize that they weren't just scattered haphazardly on the floor. Instead, they were in neat piles, forming a kind of mind map for a story. Maya started to move through the piles, reading papers as she went.

They mostly seemed to be articles on the Moonlight Killer, but it was more complex than that. Each pile seemed to represent one of his victims, everything there connected to them. And it wasn't just the ones he'd killed. Maya quickly spotted a pile with her sister's photograph near the top, containing everything from printed copies of some of her artworks to articles speculating about what she might be doing now.

A more general pile seemed to be dedicated just to Francis Hanratty and his background. There was a notepad next to it, which Maya flicked through in the hope of finding some message there between them, some hint that Lisa might be taking instructions from him. Instead, all she found was a series of notes proclaiming Hanratty's brilliance, the ease with which he'd killed. There were ramblings trying to understand the same "message" that Lisa had talked about back in the interrogation room.

What there wasn't was any smoking gun. Maya moved through to the bedroom, looking for anything that might link her directly to the crimes. The killer was using wire garrotes. Those were potentially distinctive, so if Maya could find them here, that would be all the proof she needed, but it would also be good enough to prove a link if she found trophies taken from the victims, or planning for their murders, anything that couldn't just be written off as obsession.

She started to search, checking drawers, looking under the bed, checking for loose floorboards or carefully constructed hiding spaces. Maya could feel her frustration growing as she found nothing. No sign of anything that might link Lisa Franklin to the three murders so far. She checked for bloodstained clothing in the laundry basket, but there was nothing incriminating there, either.

"Is there anything on the computer?" Maya asked Marco, heading back into the living area of the apartment.

"Nothing that would be enough for a jury."

Which meant that they had nothing. Maya considered what that meant.

"It's possible that she's not the killer," she said.

Marco looked as frustrated as Maya felt. He gestured to the neat piles on the floor. "Someone who's *this* obsessed with the Moonlight Killer, but she's not doing this?"

"In some ways, her obsession counts against her being the killer," Maya said. "She would know that Francis Hanratty *hates* copycats. And if she were determined to copy him anyway, she would get the details right. Come on, we should head back to the station. Bring the notes. There might be something in them."

They left the apartment, locking it behind them and heading back to the car. On the drive back, Maya tried to think of anything else that might connect Lisa Franklin to the case, or, failing that, anything that might give them a way into the case.

The trouble was, Maya was coming up empty. The physical evidence didn't lead them anywhere obvious, while the connection between the victims was too broad to be useful. By the time she and Marco reached the Miltonberg PD, she was fuming with frustration.

Officer Bryant met them as they went into the lobby of the police department. It was almost empty at that time of day, with just a couple of cops booking in a drunk. "Find anything?"

Maya shook her head. "Nothing directly incriminating, although there's plenty that suggests she's obsessed with the Moonlight Killer. I get the feeling that if Francis Hanratty ever *did* tell her to do something, she wouldn't hesitate for a moment. But that's not enough to hold her. We'll have to let her go, Bryant, but you should probably keep an eye on her from now on."

"Don't worry," Bryant said. "We will. If our resident reporter decides to start helping that psycho, we'll be there."

Maya hoped so. She headed in the direction of the interrogation room, where Lisa Franklin was sitting with an older woman in a suit who Maya assumed was her lawyer. That suspicion was confirmed the moment that she walked into the room.

“This is intolerable,” the lawyer said. “My client has been kept waiting in here for more than an hour, after being wrongfully arrested. I demand that you let her go at once.”

“That’s what I came in here to do,” Maya said. “You’re free to go, Lisa. Although I suggest you find someone healthier to obsess over. I’ve met Frank Hanratty, and if he ever meets *you*, he’ll probably kill you.”

“I’m not sure you really understand him, even now,” Lisa said, as she started for the door. “No hard feelings though, Agent Gray? After all, when all of this is done, I’m going to have the biggest story that Miltonberg has ever seen because of you.”

Maya let her go. She was delusional and obsessive, not the killer. Of course, that thought made dread start to fill Maya once again, because if they didn’t have the killer in custody, he or she was still out there somewhere, and they might already be searching for their next victim.

CHAPTER TWENTY

The best thing about taking a sabbatical from the university, Jordan Clarke decided, was that it finally gave him a chance to unwind after so many years of working steadily, plugging away at making progress in his career.

He lay down on the weights bench, pushing his curly black hair away from his rounded features before reaching up for the bar above. He grunted with effort as he lifted the stacked barbell once, twice, a third time. Not bad for a man of forty-eight.

As he sat up to take a rest following the set, he decided that actually, the *best* part was knowing that all of his colleagues would still be working hard, setting papers, marking exams, stuck in the library as they tried to squeeze some fresh iota of knowledge from their field. Jordan hadn't been in the library in a week and, if he went back in there, it wouldn't be crammed in between tutorials.

Lying back down, Jordan started to pump out his second set, music turned up loud. Eighties metal, of course, proper lifting music, not any of this modern rubbish. Another contender for the best thing about all of this: he could blast the music as loud as he wanted, given that he was home in the middle of the day. There was a time when his wife might have complained about it, but Janet leaving him was one of the reasons he'd decided to take the sabbatical in the first place.

At least he knew a good lawyer, Jordan thought with a smirk. Plenty of them, given that he was a law professor, although his specialism tended to be wrongful convictions rather than divorce law. Still, one of his old students had remembered Jordan fondly enough to help him out, which meant that at least he got to keep the house.

As for his job… well, he had tenure, he could do pretty much what he wanted. Up to and including taking a year's sabbatical. Jordan forced his way through his second set on the bench, before heading back into the house to grab some cranberry juice from the refrigerator.

While he was in there, Jordan toweled down briefly and went through into his study, crammed with law books. His computer sat there, dark and lifeless for the moment, as it had been for days now.

Another good thing about being on sabbatical: not having to answer endless emails from the university administration.

Jordan had a theory about university administrators, which was that they weren't really necessary above a certain base level, and they knew it. To disguise that fact, they had to fill the world with paperwork that only they understood, with academic emergencies and urgent emails in an environment that really should never have done urgency at all. They created artificial pressure, because if they didn't, people might work out that they didn't really matter.

Jordan didn't switch the computer on, but he did sit and make a few notes for his upcoming trip. After all, there wasn't much point to a sabbatical if all he was going to do for a whole year was sit at home.

No, Jordan would finally get to do the kind of research that he wanted. He would head out around the country, talking to people who had been wrongfully convicted, but also the people who had helped to put them there: the cops who just wanted a result regardless of whether it was the right one, the forensics experts using cutting edge techniques that proved to be no better than guesswork, the eye-witnesses who thought that they'd seen one thing when in fact they'd seen another. Going around collecting data that way, he would have the makings of a seminal book on all the ways that the law could go wrong for people, all the ways that innocent men and women could find themselves scooped up by the grasp of the justice system, never to be let go.

Maybe he could actually make a difference.

At the very least, he would get some of his colleagues off his back about publishing so infrequently since he'd gotten tenure. He knew what they thought: that old Prof. Clarke had gone soft, that he'd lost the fire to fight for justice!

Well, probably they'd been right, but there was nothing like a divorce to revitalize a guy. He'd started working out. He would write his magnum opus. Maybe he would even put in some pro bono work fighting for those who didn't have the money to appeal against their convictions along the way. Although he would have to find a way to fit that around the travelling.

He'd already started to put his foot back into the publishing waters with his paper on the Francis Hanratty case, about why this killer had probably been convicted of the wrong number of crimes, and why injustice mattered even against the worst in society. It had seemed like a good way to get the old argumentative muscles back in shape, and if it grabbed a little attention for his next project, all the better.

Jordan heard a crash from back in the garage, and for a second he jumped. He went through and saw that his barbell had toppled sideways from the weights bench, crashing into the floor of the garage. Jordan reminded himself that really, he should replace his weights whenever he wasn't using them to avoid that kind of thing happening. He bent over, starting to remove the weights from the bar, putting them back on their rack. When he was finally done, he stretched out slightly and headed over to the spot where he'd hung a punch bag, throwing on wraps and gloves then starting to attack it.

Jordan had seen his share of trouble over the years. Not everyone appreciated a law professor coming around, trying to tell them that a conviction should be overturned. More than one family member of a victim had tried to attack him, not understanding that, every day the wrong person was in prison meant that the actual wrongdoer was still out there somewhere. Of course, there were cases where there was no other obvious suspect, but that wasn't Jordan's fault. It simply meant that law enforcement hadn't done their job well enough.

Jordan turned up the music and kept punching. He had a date tonight, the first for a while. He would need to be ready in plenty of time. For now, though, he wanted to be pumped. He wanted the kind of adrenaline rush that a life in academia so rarely provided.

Jordan saw something flicker through his field of vision. He had a moment of confusion about what it might be, but then something sharp and biting snapped tight around his throat, a foot kicking at the back of his knee to bring him down.

Jordan tried to fight back, tried to struggle, but in that moment, he couldn't think of a single thing to do that might help. He scrabbled at the wire cutting into his neck, gasping for air even as blackness closed in around him. He was on the ground now, and still someone was pulling the wire tighter.

Jordan was still trying to pull the wire away when the blackness claimed him for good.

CHAPTER TWENTY ONE

The university campus looked peaceful as Maya and Marco walked through it, but she could feel the tension running underneath it all. Students moved quickly between lectures and the library, not hanging around and talking the way the normally would have. Maya saw professors looking around warily, as if afraid that someone might attack them at any moment.

Maya guessed that the only reason any classes were still running was that most of the people on campus had no reason to be afraid. So far, the killer had shown no signs of wanting to attack students, and the only staff members they had targeted had been ones who had done work on the Moonlight Killer case in the town. In theory, most of the people there should have been in no danger at all, but that didn't stop an atmosphere of fear from pervading the campus.

Maya suspected that nothing would until she and Marco found the killer and put an end to this.

"Why did you want to come back to the campus?" Marco asked, looking around at the students, the tree lined courtyards, the ivy clad buildings. "We could have kept working the files in the local PD."

Maya nodded. She knew that. It was just that she felt that there was more to be gained here.

"This feels like the heart of it all," she said. "The killer could be targeting people anywhere in the town. He could have chosen Lisa Franklin as a victim, given how much she's written on the Moonlight Killer. He could have come after you or me, given the role we played in tracking down Hanratty. But he didn't. He's chosen to focus on academics. There's something here, in the college, that's important to this case."

"Okay, I get that," Marco replied. "But what? We already looked at the possibility of academic rivalry being behind this, or someone obsessed with the old Moonlight Killer case. What does that leave?"

That was the part that was proving elusive. Maya had no doubt that the Moonlight Killer case was at the heart of this, but simply knowing that didn't get them anywhere. It didn't point to an obvious suspect, although in Lisa Franklin's case it had helped to confirm her as one. It didn't even really tell Maya what all of this was about. Why did someone *care* that these academics were writing about the Moonlight Killer? Was this all about some follower of Francis Hanratty who thought that they were defaming him in their work? Someone connected to a victim who thought that they were glorifying him, somehow? Someone engaged in the field on an academic level who wanted to eliminate the competition?

"There are still plenty of options," Maya said. "Let's start by checking in with the grad students we borrowed. They may have had time to find something by now."

Marco nodded, and the two of them headed in the direction of the criminology department and the office where Prof. Nieman's grad students were working to build up profiles of their fellow students. One was a young man with a busy blonde beard and blue eyes, wearing a shirt, waistcoat and slacks. The other was an Arab-American young woman wearing dark jeans and a t-shirt for some band Maya had never heard of.

"You must be Nicholas and Zia," Maya said. "I'm Agent Gray, this is Agent Spinelli."

"You want to know how the profiles are coming along?" Zia said.

Maya nodded. "Is there anyone who obviously stands out?"

The younger woman shook her head. "Not so far, at least, not as far as we can see. We're still running additional layers of analysis, but at first glance… nothing. Maybe the stats will give us more."

The young man winced. "Save us from statistics driven objectivism. We both know that simple numbers couldn't have predicted *any* of the major killers of the twentieth century."

"So you say, Nicholas. I still think that when my modelling is finished for my doctorate..."

"*If* it's ever finished."

It sounded like an old argument between them. Maya coughed, interrupting.

"We're grateful for any further analysis you want to do," she said. "But right now, I just need to know if there's anyone who has liked a bunch of posts about the Moonlight Killer, or who seems obsessed with him, or who has started talking about how they could have committed his murders better. Anything like that?"

Both grad students shook their heads simultaneously.

"If there were someone who stood out that much," Nicholas said. "We would have called you by now."

"What about anyone who just comes across as creepy?" Marco asked. "Forget what's in the data; presumably you've met a lot of these kids. Is there anyone people avoid? Anyone people just *know* there's something wrong about?"

"Ah," Nicholas said. "You're referring, of course, to the current theory that it may be possible to spot psychopaths by looking at just pictures or short video clips of them?"

"Sure," Marco said.

"Well, even I have to admit that method is a long way from foolproof."

"And we wouldn't want the FBI going after people based on just the 'vibe' they get from them," Zia added. "That opens up the way to all kinds of wrongful arrests."

Maya understood that. She also knew just how good some serial killers could be at hiding behind a façade of charm. Even so, she wondered if there was an answer to Marco's question.

"*Is* there anyone like that, though?" she asked.

Again, though, the grad students shook their heads.

"Not that we know of," Nicholas said. "We'll keep looking through the list, trying to identify anyone who is hiding what they're doing better."

Maya was grateful for that, although she did wonder if the grad student was doing it because he really thought that he might find something, or just to keep being useful to the FBI.

Maya looked across to Marco, who shrugged. It seemed that he didn't have anything else to ask here. The two of them turned for the door, but Zia called out to them.

"There is *one* other thing," she said.

Maya turned back to her. "Something to do with the students?"

Zia shook her head. "This is connected to the list of people working on Moonlight Killer related research. We have the list from the dean based on the people who responded to his email, but I think there's a name missing."

That was enough to catch Maya's attention.

"What name?"

"Prof. Jordan Clarke," Zia said. "He's a law professor at the university. I was at a talk he gave last year about wrongful convictions, and he was using the Moonlight Killer as one of his examples, showing how the police and FBI had assumed that every killing that looked vaguely like one of his *was* one of his."

That was a problem that Maya had run into throughout the cases the Moonlight Killer had forced her to work. He'd wanted her to set the record straight, had forced her to find other killers to prove that he didn't commit many of the crimes that were attributed to him.

"Why wouldn't he reply to the email?" Maya wondered aloud.

"Well, I think he's on sabbatical," Zia said. "So maybe he isn't checking his university email?"

If not, then he might not know the danger he was potentially in. Maya started back towards the door, hurrying now.

"I'll get an address for the professor," she said. "You drive. We need to warn him about what's going on."

***

Prof. Jordan Clarke's home was a small place a little way from the campus. It was a neat little house in the middle of a square of lawn, with a driveway leading up to a garage at the side of the house.

Would the professor be in? He wasn't answering the phone number Maya had been able to find for him, but that might just mean that he didn't want to answer calls from a strange number.

"We don't have any reason to think that he's in danger," Marco said.

"Except that he's done academic work on the Moonlight Killer," Maya pointed out.

"Which puts him at risk in general terms, but we don't know that there's a specific threat to him."

Maya nodded. She knew that, but they still needed to warn him, maybe offer him some kind of protection until they could wrap this case up. Maya also wanted to ask him a few questions to find out if he had any information about the others. Maybe he could point to an academic rival, or to some additional point of connection between the victims. Even if he wasn't in immediate danger, it was definitely worth coming out here to speak with him.

Maya got out of the car and headed for the house, with Marco trailing slightly behind her. Loud rock music was coming from the garage. Maya started to feel the hairs on the back of her neck prickling, her instincts telling her that something was wrong here. She saw the reason for that a moment later: the front door to the house was slightly open, the lock broken.

Maya drew her gun, seeing Marco do the same beside her. They slipped into the house, checking for danger.

"Professor Clarke?" Maya called out. "This is the FBI."

She hoped against hope that he would call out to them, demand to know what they were doing in his home. Instead, the music remained the only sound there. Maya started to move through the house carefully, checking every corner as she went in case there was someone hidden there, waiting to leap out. The living room and kitchen were clear.

With her hand shaking slightly, Maya opened the door to the garage. Instantly, the scent of blood assaulted her nostrils. Maya moved inside, and the sight in there was enough to make her freeze in place for a second, simply staring.

A muscular man with curly black hair and a round face hung by his wrists from a pullup bar. He'd been tied there with what appeared to be a couple of boxing hand-wraps. His eyes were open and staring, but the life had long since left them. Maya could see the silver gleam of a garotte around his throat, blood covering his shirt.

"We need to check the house and call this in," Marco said.

Maya nodded, even as she silently cursed herself. Another victim so soon, and they were still no closer to finding the killer. He could be anyone, could be anywhere. She hated that, and it also made her afraid.

What were they missing, and who would he target next?

CHAPTER TWENTY TWO

"Why are we not getting anywhere?" Maya demanded, as she and Marco sat in their borrowed office. "It feels as though we're just running from connection to connection in this case, with no actual answers."

Another death, and it gave them no new information, no new forensics.

Marco spread his hands. "We're dealing with a killer who's being careful, who isn't leaving us evidence. With someone like that, all we *can* do is look for whatever connections we can find."

Maya knew that, but it didn't make it any easier to take. She sighed, looking over at Marco. They were both tired by this point, but Maya could see the determination on Marco's face. She knew he wasn't going to give up and that he would be beside her every step of the way on this. Maya was more than grateful for that.

Marco moved over to her, massaging some of the tension out of Maya's shoulders with sure, steady hands. Maya sank into that touch, glad that she had him there with her, glad that she had the comfort of the man she loved beside her on this. She leaned up to kiss him…

That was when her phone went off, making Maya jump. She hadn't realized that this case had gotten her nerves wound so tightly. A part of her was already wondering if there might be yet another victim in this case when she saw Agent Swift's name on the screen.

Maya picked up.

"Gray," Swift said without preamble. "Progress report."

"We've established that the victims in this case all researched the Moonlight Killer in some way," Maya said. "But the M.O. is too different for it to be him. We've identified at least one person obsessed with the Moonlight Killer, but we don't think she's in the frame for this. We're still working on the information we have, hoping it will lead us somewhere new."

"In other words, you aren't making progress," Swift said, with no give in her voice. "And in the meantime, I'm hearing reports of more deaths. Do I need to come down there to take over this case, Gray?"

"No ma'am," Maya said. "Deputy Director, how is the hunt for Francis Hanratty coming?"

"You focus on your case," Swift replied. "We'll handle things here."

She hung up.

That said to Maya that Swift wasn't making much progress at her end either, because if they were on the verge of catching him, Maya had no doubt that Swift would want to emphasize how much they'd achieved without Maya or Marco. It was frustrating, though, to be left out of the loop when the killer who had kidnapped her sister and so many other women was still on the loose.

"I take it Swift wasn't happy?" Marco said.

Maya shook her head. Deputy Director Swift was a woman who valued results above everything.

"Is there anything new in the coroner's report or the forensics for this murder?" Maya asked.

Marco went back to his desk, looking at the files. "Not that I can see. The method of killing is the same: a wire garotte that both strangled Jordan Clarke and cut into his throat. He was posed post mortem, the way the others were. Some signs that Jordan tried to struggle, but no major bruising that would indicate a long fight. Forensics say that there are no fingerprints. They have plenty of blood samples to test, but they suspect that they'll turn out to all be from the victim."

"See if they can rush the results just in case," Maya said. There was always a chance that the killer had managed to cut himself on his own wire weapon. If so, they would have the DNA they needed to identify him.

In the meantime, Maya needed a way into this case that wasn't reliant on the forensic evidence. She'd already looked at the connections between the victims, so was there anything else to find by looking in that direction?

"When I've talked to forensics, I'll look deeper into the professor," Marco said. "Maybe there will be something there that will help us to make more sense of what's going on here."

The problem was that Maya already had the feeling that they *knew* what was going on here. This was about the Moonlight Killer, even if the evidence suggested that he hadn't been directly involved in the killings. Could he be directing them somehow? Could he be instructing someone to kill in a way that was close to his old M.O., but which did not copy it completely?

That seemed possible. At the very least, it seemed to Maya that they were looking for someone obsessed with the serial killer, someone who wanted to target people who had written about him in order to establish some kind of twisted connection to the killer in their mind.

Maya's thoughts drifted back to Lisa Franklin. While it now seemed clear to her that the reporter wasn't behind the killings, they were looking for someone at least that obsessed.

Thoughts of Lisa made Maya think of the stacks of notes that they'd taken as evidence from Lisa's apartment. Lisa Franklin had been looking into the Moonlight Killer in the context of Miltonberg for a long time. Maybe she had spotted something that wouldn't be apparent to Maya or Marco?

Maya grabbed the first of those boxes of notes, starting to sort through them. Some of the notes were small things: hints about times and places relating to that first death in the city at the Moonlight Killer's hands. There was a note about a potential sighting of the killer by a diner, a detailed analysis of the injuries to the victim, a report that looked as if it had been obtained from the local police.

There were many more general notes about Francis Hanratty, obviously made since his conviction as the Moonlight Killer. There was a whole section on his past, including a couple of interviews with people he'd grown up alongside.

There were notes on local figures, of such depth that Maya might have reconsidered Lisa as a suspect, simply for the intrusiveness of them. Her notes for the professors she'd interviewed included the details of their lives and side notes such as:

I don't think MK would like Prof. Hart's work. It characterizes him too simply. It ignores the full complexity of what he is trying to do.

Maya kept reading, kept trying to make some sense of the file. She felt as though she was getting at least as much of an insight into Lisa Franklin's mind as that of Francis Hanratty, and what she saw there was worrying. This was someone who talked about a serial killer like a hero, who wondered what it would take to get to speak to him, what he would ask of her, and how easy it would be to do.

Maya found her eye caught by notes on someone else, a man named Richard Ames. Maya frowned as she saw the sheer volume of notes on him: several pages, all filled with details and pictures. It seemed as if Lisa were producing a profile on him, ready for some kind of interview.

A few words, underlined, stood out to Maya: *Possible follower of MK?*

Those words made Maya stop in her tracks, starting to read that section of the files over again, determined to learn as much as she could about Richard Ames. He was, according to Lisa's notes, a security consultant there in Miltonberg, who had helped to put in the security systems for the campus. Other notes suggested that he occasionally worked as private security for less savory characters. There was a picture of him in the file: a man in his forties, with buzz cut hair, tinged with Gray. Lisa's notes suggested that he had a military background, although he'd been thrown out for getting into fights on base.

Maya stared as she saw that another photograph showed a partial image of a tattoo: a snake eating an armadillo under a full moon. The potential meaning of that wasn't lost on her. Did that mean that he'd been in the same unit as Hanratty? Or did it just mean that he was so obsessed with the Moonlight Killer that he'd gotten the same tattoo? Either way, it implied the kind of connection that made her shudder. Was it possible that this man was working for Hanratty?

The section that really made Maya stop and stare was about the Moonlight Killer's escape. Lisa noted that Richard had been out of town that night, and a friend of hers at a credit card company had supplied details of a transaction at a gas station just a couple of miles from where the prison van had been hit. Had he really played some role in the Moonlight Killer's escape?

That couldn't just be coincidence. Could it?

"Marco, come look at this," Maya said, spreading the pages out over the desk. "Tell me what you make of it."

She watched Marco read through it slowly, his frown deepening as he went.

"She had all this but didn't report any of it?" he said.

Maya nodded. Lisa was going to be in a lot of trouble for that. "And Ames? What do you make of him?"

Marco considered it for another second or two. "I think we just found our killer."

CHAPTER TWENTY THREE

Maya stared at Richard Ames home through the sights of her rifle, trying to get any intel she could on the layout before she and Marco went in. She knew how dangerous this moment was, so she was determined not to take any chances.

The house was slightly outside of Miltonberg, an old farmhouse that reminded Maya far too much of the place where Francis Hanratty had grown up. There were several outbuildings while an SUV stood waiting in the middle of the farmyard.

"I can see cameras on the corners," Maya said, lowering the rifle to rest against her tactical vest. "My guess is that there will be motion sensors too. Do you have the warrant?"

"Right here," Marco said, holding it up. He was wearing a tactical vest of his own and carrying a shotgun. Maya hoped that it would be enough to keep him safe. The thought of anything happening to him was almost too much to bear. "Are you sure you don't want to bring the local cops in on this?"

Maya shook her head. "That's not a situation we can control. We don't know how they'll react under fire. I could turn this into a bloodbath. It's better if we go in, take down Ames, and then bring them in to help with the search and forensics."

Marco considered that for a moment. "All right, but how do we handle this, just the two of us? If we drive up, he'll see us coming and either destroy any evidence or run."

That was Maya's worry, too, but she had a third option in her mind. If Richard Ames saw them coming, he might try to fight them, might try to kill them both. That was why they were both dressed for a tactical assault, and why they would be approaching this cautiously.

"We'll make our way to the farmhouse on foot," Maya said. She looked through her scope again. "I can see movement there in the living room, front right as we're looking now. We'll head there through that stand of trees, work our way around the house and enter through the front. I don't think there's any way to avoid the cameras once we're in the yard, so we'll have to move quickly once we're there."

It was the best chance they had of getting to Ames before he could escape or prepare to fight back. Even then, Maya expected him to run for a weapon. They had to be prepared for a fight from the moment they entered the farmhouse.

Maya led the way, out around the perimeter of the property, with Marco following close behind. There was no one else she trusted to have her back the way she did with him. It felt good to have that backup now, even as she worried about whether this would get Marco hurt.

Maya knew that she shouldn't worry like that. He was a trained FBI agent and had been a cop before that. But it was hard not to worry when going into a situation like this with someone she cared about so much.

"Ready?" she asked, as they reached a spot where Maya thought that they could enter the property unseen.

"Ready," Marco assured her.

Maya crossed the fence line, then paused, just a yard inside the perimeter. She saw the tripwire there, which might be linked to an alarm, or to something far worse. Carefully, Maya crouched and cut it, moving forward into the trees.

She moved through them cautiously, watching for any other tripwires or traps. She spotted one motion sensor hung up in the trees and carefully avoided it, keeping going. Marco was following exactly in her footsteps. That was good. Somewhere like this, even one pace off the trail she knew to be safe might put them both in danger.

They emerged from the trees, with the house just ahead. There was no way to do this part slowly.

"Go!" Maya said, hurrying for the door. She could feel her heart pounding as she did it, the adrenaline rushing through her veins. She knew that if Richard Ames had seen them coming, he might have had time to take cover in one of the surrounding buildings with a weapon. He might be waiting to pick them off, even now. Even as she ran for the door, Maya scanned the surrounding area for threats, and tried to work out where she would dive for cover.

No shots came, though. She and Marco arrived at the front door to Ames' house without coming under attack. Maybe he was waiting there, deciding that this would be the best place to make a stand. Maya had no doubt that alarms would be sounding inside by now. There was no more time to waste.

She stepped aside, letting Marco kick the door, his larger frame putting more weight behind the movement. It resisted one kick, but on the second, the wood around the lock splintered, letting the door fly open to give them a way inside.

"Richard Ames!" Maya called out, as they burst into a hallway lined with pictures of Ames in what appeared to be various war zones, protecting important figures. "This is the FBI! We have a warrant for your arrest! Come out with your hands behind your head!"

Maya expected that announcement to be met by gunfire, but there was nothing. She and Marco hurried through the house, heading for the living room where she had seen movement before.

It was sleek and modern, a clear contrast to the more rural surroundings. A bank of computers had been set up in one corner, several screens watching the world around the farm. There was a cork board on one side of the room, with pictures of the victims to date on it, along with newspaper clippings. A wire garrote lay on a table in front of it.

Richard Ames was standing in the middle of the room next to a single leather armchair. He was dressed in black slacks and a dark polo neck sweater. It added to the sense of menace that exuded from the man.

Too late, Maya saw that he had some kind of device in his hand. He pressed a button on it, and a loud bang punctuated the silence of the room. Smoke started to pour from the casings of the computers in the corner.

"Hands up, Ames!" Marco ordered. "Drop that and show me your hands."

Maya tensed, her weapon trained on the security consultant. She could feel a bead of sweat running down her brow. She expected that, at any moment, Ames would reach for a weapon. She readied herself to fire, readied herself to take down the man who seemed to have killed so many people.

Instead, Ames put his hands behind his head and sank to his knees smoothly, giving no sign of resistance.

"I'll cover him," Maya said. "Cuff him."

Marco nodded and moved behind Richard Ames. Even now, Maya expected him to try to lash out, for this all to be a trick to lure Marco closer. She could see the caution in Marco's movements too, could see that he was thinking the same thing. Instead, Ames allowed Marco to cuff him without any resistance and read him his rights.

"You've been working for the Moonlight Killer," Maya said.

Ames smiled up at her. "*With*. Not for. He chooses those who are special, those who have talent."

That willingness to admit to it caught Maya by surprise. If Ames really was everything he appeared to be, then she expected to be met by a wall of silence, a desire to give nothing away. The fact that he'd trashed the computers said that he was intent on hiding at least some parts of what he knew.

"And it's because of him that you've been killing academics?" Marco said.

Ames smiled. "They deserved to die. Every last one of them, for the falsehoods they uttered about *him*."

There was the kind of fervor in his eyes that Maya might have expected from some kind of cult member. Richard Ames appeared to be admitting to the murders. There was a wire garotte on the table that would presumably have his DNA on it. Everything appeared to be finished, wrapped up neatly.

So why couldn't Maya shake the feeling that there was still something else going on here?

CHAPTER TWENTY FOUR

"Ames doesn't want a lawyer," Marco said, stepping out of the interrogation room at the Miltonberg PD.

Maya stared into it through the one-way mirror dividing it from the small observation room in which she sat. Richard Ames was sitting calmly, his expression almost empty. He didn't seem to care that he was in custody, although, to Maya, that lack of care seemed forced. She could see the faint twitch in one eye that betrayed deeper emotions.

"Doesn't that strike you as strange?" Maya said. "A man like Richard Ames should lawyer up the moment we get him in here, then refuse to say anything. He shouldn't just sit there and wait to talk to us."

"Maybe he's treating this like some military interrogation," Marco suggested. "Just deciding not to say anything."

Maya wasn't sure that she believed that, either. There was something else going on here. She just couldn't work out what, exactly.

"We need to get in there to talk to him," Maya said.

Marco nodded. "How do you want to approach this? I get the feeling that 'good cop, bad cop' isn't going to work on a guy like this."

"Then we don't play that kind of game with him," Maya said. "I think, with Richard Ames, we have to be cleverer than that."

She headed into the interrogation room, with Marco alongside her. They both took seats opposite Ames and his eyes flickered over each of them in turn. His expression mostly showed contempt, but Maya thought that she saw a hint of something else there under the surface too as his eyes flickered away from them, she saw the sweat on his brow.

Richard Ames was afraid and trying not to show it.

"So," Maya said. "You know who we are, Richard?"

He nodded. "Maya Gray and Marco Spinelli. *He* talks a lot about you."

"So you admit that you're in contact with Francis Hanratty?" Marco asked.

Ames shrugged. "How else am I meant to hear the purity of his message?"

"And what message is that?" Maya asked.

"That the strong take from the weak. That the whole world is designed to hold back people like us. Designed to constrain us, control us."

Maya raised an eyebrow. That wasn't quite the same message as the one Lisa Franklin had assumed. Did that mean that she didn't know the truth, or did it just mean that Hanratty adjusted what he was saying to suit his audience? Maya was willing to bet that it was the latter. He was good at manipulating people, good at getting them to do what he wanted.

"So, you think you're the same as him?" Maya asked.

"You think I'm not?" Ames snapped back, anger filling his eyes. "You think I wouldn't hunt you down and make you beg for death, given the chance?"

"Why haven't you, then?" Maya asked.

Ames looked briefly puzzled.

"Why haven't you?" Maya repeated. "You must have known that we were in town almost from the moment we arrived. Lisa Franklin probably told you, for one thing."

"Her?" Ames said in a mocking tone. "She's a hanger on. She likes the mystique of it all, but she doesn't have what it takes to actually *do* anything."

"But you *have* been talking with her, haven't you?" Marco asked.

Ames shrugged. "She gives me information. She asks me questions. When I feel like it, I answer her. She thinks she knows about Frank. She doesn't."

"And you do?" Maya said. "Oh yes, because you're the same as him, aren't you?"

Richard Ames glared at her then. "If he hadn't told me to keep my distance, I would have killed the pair of you when you came into town."

Maya considered that. She should have felt afraid, should have felt her breathing coming faster, her heart starting to pound in her chest. Instead, she just looked at Ames levelly.

"But you didn't, because you take orders," Maya said. "Because really, you're just a follower, aren't you? I've talked to Francis. We've interrogated him. I know how cold he is. I'm not sure he even feels anything when he kills. He certainly wouldn't be sitting here, afraid."

"You think I'm afraid?" Ames surged up from the table, but his cuffs held him back. Maya very deliberately didn't react.

"Where is he now?" Marco asked.

Ames shook his head. "I wouldn't tell you if I knew."

"But you *don't* know?" Maya asked.

That got a flicker of reaction from the security consultant.

"It's about operational security. You can't make me tell you what I don't know."

Maya smiled slightly. "So, he expected that you would be caught here? You were that expendable to him?"

"That's not how it was!" Ames snapped, in another angry outburst.

"He doesn't care about you," Maya said. "Michael Francis Hanratty is incapable of caring about anyone."

Ames was shaking his head even before Maya finished the sentence. "He shows us the way. He helps us to plan. When one of us wants to act, he shows us the way to do it."

"He shows you how to get away with murder?" Marco asked.

Ames settled back into his seat, staring at the two of them without answering.

"Did he send you to kill the academics?" Maya asked.

"They deserved to die," Ames replied.

"That's not an answer," Maya said, but Ames didn't say any more than that. He stared at her instead.

"You must see how this is going to go," Marco said. "Four people dead at the hands of someone copying the Moonlight Killer. Now we find you, one of his followers, with a weapon identical to the one used to kill them? Your only hope is to start talking. Give us Hanratty, and it will work in your favor."

Ames sat there, staring straight ahead. Maya could see the fear in him, though, the worry.

"I don't care what you do to me. Charge me with their murders, I don't care. I'm not saying another word."

He fell silent and Maya glanced across to Marco, gesturing to the door. Marco nodded and the two of them headed from the room, giving Richard Ames some time to stew.

"He'll talk," Marco said once they were back in the observation room, looking through the glass at him. "Sooner or later, he'll tell us something."

"Maybe," Maya said. "Although my guess is that what he was saying is true: he doesn't know much about where Hanratty is at the moment. I'm more worried about the fact that he hasn't *quite* confessed to any of the murders."

Marco gave her a puzzled look. "That doesn't mean he's innocent. And he's all but confessed."

"He's said that the victims deserved to die. He's said that he would like to kill the two of us. He hasn't come out and said that he killed the four victims." To Maya, it was an important distinction.

Marco clearly didn't feel the same way. "There was an example of the murder weapon right there in his house."

"Just one," Maya pointed out. "I would expect this killer to have a whole stock of garrotes waiting for him to use them."

"He had the victims' pictures up on a board, like he was stalking them," Marco pointed out.

"Or as if he were looking into their deaths," Maya said. "Maybe tracking our investigation. We *know* that Hanratty likes to watch us. Maybe this is the only way he can, now."

"Or maybe Richard Ames is just the killer," Marco suggested. "Maybe we don't need to overcomplicate this, Maya. Hanratty sent him to kill people who were talking about him. He butchered them, just like his boss would have."

"That's the thing, Marco," Maya said. "Ames doesn't *feel* the same as Hanratty. He's not cold in the same way. He feels as though he *wants* to be a killer, as if he wants to be the same, but he's not the same kind of psychopath."

Marco shook his head. "That's not enough, Maya. A man like this, here and now… he must be the killer. And if he isn't, then why isn't he denying it outright?"

Maya considered that. "Maybe he just wants to make sure that *someone* goes down for this crime. Maybe, if he persuades us that he's responsible for these four, we'll think he committed the other murder in the town, and the Moonlight Killer's tally gets scrubbed of another crime he doesn't want to claim."

"You think that someone would take the fall for murder, just so that Hanratty can claim only the kills he wants?" Marco asked, sounding disbelieving.

"I think that Francis Hanratty is capable of manipulating people into doing just about anything," Maya replied. "And Ames comes across as a fanatic. Yes, I think he'd go to prison for this, regardless of whether he did it."

Marco stood there, obviously thinking about it for several seconds. Finally, he shook his head.

"I'm sorry, Maya, but I don't buy it. Look, I'm going to go back in there. If I get a full confession out of him, will *that* put your mind at rest?"

Maya wasn't sure even that would right then. She just wasn't sure that Richard Ames was the killer, and if that was the case, then the real killer was still out there somewhere, possibly getting ready to strike again.

CHAPTER TWENTY FIVE

He waited carefully outside the building that housed the recording studio, listening to Melissa Turner talking about her favorite topic: the Moonlight Killer.

"By this point, it seems pretty obvious that all of these murders are connected to the Moonlight Killer somehow, going right back to that original kill in the park," she said. "So now, what we have to ask is *how* the murders are connected. Is this a fresh spree by the Moonlight Killer? Is it a copycat? How do we go about deciding?"

Melissa was a teaching assistant at the college. Another academic with opinions on that first death. Another person spreading lies to the world at large. Lies he'd decided he couldn't let stand.

In one sense, it was his own fault. He'd made that one kill look too much like the Moonlight Killer's work. He'd taken the time to get the details right, partly hoping that it would disguise what he was doing, partly thinking that it might be an interesting nod to another killer's work. But then, he'd done it too well, disguising his efforts so effectively that even the FBI attributed *his* kill to another man.

"I can see in the chat that some of you are wondering whether I'm worried, talking about the Moonlight Killer when so many others who have done that are dead," Melissa said. "And look, it's great that everyone is so concerned for me, and I understand the seriousness of the situation. I knew so many of the professors who have died, and I don't want to trivialize what happened to them, not for one moment."

She paused for a moment, and he got the sense that she was trying to marshal her arguments, making sure that she said the right things.

"But look, we have to remember that I'm not a full professor. I'm just a TA, so I probably wouldn't fit the pattern anyway. And then there's the news I've been seeing on my feeds that the FBI have brought someone in for this. There hasn't been an official announcement yet, but everyone is saying that they've caught the killer. That Miltonberg is… well, as safe as it has ever been."

He stopped short at those words, feeling a wash of shock and anger. The FBI thought that they'd caught the killer. Another killer, another *pretender,* was getting the credit for his work.

In the first couple of months after the kill where he'd copied the Moonlight Killer's method, it had seemed like such a good idea. The Moonlight Killer was already known to be unknowable, unfindable, to operate anywhere and everywhere. There was no reason why anyone would continue to search in or around Miltonberg. There was no reason why anyone would find *him* when they were looking for someone else.

In that, he prided himself on the ease with which he'd gotten away with his crime. By changing his pattern, mixing up what he did, he could kill whoever he wanted and it looked like nothing more than a grisly, one off murder.

For a while, he'd leaned into that. He'd traveled the country, taking a victim here, a victim there. He'd made sure that no two kills were the same. He'd shot a man in Canada, poisoned a woman in Florida, stabbed a couple out in Texas. There had been a kind of joy in that anonymity.

"Because the killer has been caught, we'll be doing a special episode on the case next week," Melissa said. "We'll be delving into his motivations, as well as into the evidence that eventually led to his capture. We'll be asking the question: is this just a cheap copycat of the Moonlight Killer, or is it something more?"

Those words made him angry. They made him want to hurt her even more. He took a couple of calming breaths. That would come soon enough.

He waited for the podcast to finish, waited for her to come down and leave the building. As always, when he saw her, he couldn't help but stare. She was in her twenties, with straight red hair and freckles, high cheekbones and deep green eyes. Whenever he saw her, his mind flashed back to another young woman, one he'd left to die arranged very carefully, very publicly. One he'd killed before the idea of copying the Moonlight Killer had ever entered his head.

That idea had probably saved him, by making sure that he didn't draw the attention of the police, but it had also doomed him, because it meant that the world had never heard of what he'd done. Even that first kill, with its beautiful artistry, had been forgotten about.

Which was why he planned to recreate it.

With the others, he'd worked quickly. He'd chosen a consistent method because he'd wanted people to see that this was all the work of one man. He'd chosen something that wasn't quite the same as the Moonlight Killer's method, because he'd wanted them to realize that the kill in the park hadn't been down to that pretender either.

Now, though, he wanted to do something different. He'd shown the world who he *wasn't*; now it was time for them to see the real face of his work.

He followed Melissa across the campus, moving calmly and quietly. He had no worries about her looking around and seeing him. He'd followed her before and she had never raised the least note of suspicion. He moved quickly and surely, not really needing to follow his target when he already knew her routine perfectly. After a podcast recording like this, she grabbed coffee, then headed for the spot where she'd locked up her bicycle for the ride back to her apartment.

He cut across to that spot now. He'd parked a van there, near the bicycles. He got in, waiting, peeking out through the window while trying to make sure that he kept low enough not to attract attention.

Doing this was an extra effort, but he wasn't afraid of effort. Part of his disdain for being mistaken for the Moonlight Killer for so long was the dawning realization that the Moonlight Killer was lazy in his kills, that he had no sense of style. As far as he could tell, the Moonlight Killer stalked his victims, killed them quickly and quietly with his strangling rope and then just… left. The Moonlight Killer didn't arrange the body, didn't take care to make sure that people saw the scene exactly as it should be.

To his mind, that missed out half the point of doing this. Why kill at all if people weren't going to find the body and be both awed and horrified by the scene they found? To him, setting the perfect moment meant at least as much as the actual instant of the kill. That was almost trivial in some ways, a thing that held power only because other people believed it to be so transgressive. There was a much greater art to be found in arranging things just so.

He saw her approaching now, and he tensed, ready for the moment when he would strike. He didn't have a wire ready for this one, not like the others. Instead, he took out a syringe, filling it carefully with the sedative he would use and waiting for Melissa to get closer, and closer. As she did so, he checked for the sight of anyone else in the area. The coast was clear; that was good.

He moved the moment she crouched to unlock her bicycle from the post it was secured to. There was no time for hesitation now. No time to pause, to have second thoughts.

He leaped out from the van, one hand reaching for her and closing over her mouth, making sure that she couldn't scream. The other hand jabbed the syringe into her neck, delivering the sedative into Melissa's bloodstream as quickly as possible. Even then, she fought, trying to wrench away his hand, trying to hit him with her elbows. It was oddly reminiscent of the way his first victim had fought so long ago.

Finally, Melissa's struggles started to ebb, her weight slumping back into him so that now he was holding her up, not holding her back. He dragged her back into the van then, closing the door behind them and starting to bind her so that she wouldn't escape even if the sedative wore off.

"You're lucky," he whispered to Melissa, not knowing if she would hear him or not. Not caring, either. "You get to live a little while longer, not like the others. Soon, though… soon, you'll pay the price for everything you've been saying."

He took a deep breath, imagining that moment.

"I'm going to make your death beautiful."

CHAPTER TWENTY SIX

The more Maya looked, the more inconsistencies she found. Richard Ames was still in the interrogation room with Marco, trying to get a confession from him, but Maya was less and less convinced that he was the killer they were looking for.

There was the single garrote, when the killer would presumably have had many to hand. There was the way his evidence board for the victims focused only on evidence gathered *after* their deaths, rather than showing the kind of planning Maya would expect from someone choosing his victims. The information there was about what had happened and the evidence there, rather than about the victims' habits and vulnerabilities.

"He's trying to find the killer," Maya said to the empty office.

Marco wasn't there to hear that conclusion, because he'd gone back into the interrogation room, but Maya was almost sure that it was true. The Moonlight Killer had always seemed to know before she did who was responsible for the crimes he sent her to investigate. Was it possible that a part of the reason for it was that he sent people to gather evidence for him? Maybe a part of the reason Richard Ames lived in Miltonberg at all was so that he could conduct some kind of long term research into the supposed Moonlight Killer murder there?

If that were true, then it suggested once again that there was still a killer out there, potentially stalking more victims while they wasted time on Ames. He was a criminal, certainly. Maybe he'd even killed elsewhere on the Moonlight Killer's orders, but Maya didn't believe that he was responsible for what was happening in the town.

Maya stood, leaving the office and making her way across the bullpen of the Miltonberg PD in the direction of the interrogation room. It seemed to her that the cops there were in a happy, even celebratory mood. It felt as if an air of tension had left the department now that Richard Ames had been brought in. Like Marco, it was obvious that they all believed that the killer was in custody.

Maya was going to have to burst that brief bubble of happiness. She was going to have to be the one to tell them all that the killer was still on the loose somewhere, and she was going to have to start by persuading Marco.

Maya was almost at the interrogation room when she saw Officer Bryant walking past, holding a file.

"What do you have there, Bryant?" Maya asked.

"Nothing to worry the FBI about," he said. "Just someone reported missing. It hasn't even been forty-eight hours yet, but a couple of the details are strange, so I thought I'd take a look."

"Who's missing?" Maya asked, feeling suddenly tense. Could this be like Evelyn Hart all over again? Was there a woman dead or dying somewhere in the city?

"A woman named Melissa Turner," Bryant said. "She's a TA at the collage, and-"

"Someone connected to the college has gone missing and you didn't *tell* me?" Maya replied instantly. Now the rising tide of worry was a tidal wave, threatening to overwhelm her.

"But you have the killer," Bryant said, with a pointed glance towards the interrogation room.

"I'm no longer sure that's the case," Maya replied, and now she saw the worry spread across Bryant's features as well.

"But… there's so much Moonlight Killer stuff in his place. I've seen what's coming back from the search team."

"He's connected to the Moonlight Killer," Maya said. "He's almost certainly guilty of a number of other crimes, including helping Francis Hanratty to escape, but that doesn't mean that he's the killer here."

She could see the realization dawning on Bryant that this wasn't the simple missing person case that he'd hoped. He handed over the file to Maya. She opened it. There was a photograph within, of a woman in her twenties with straight red hair and freckles. The photograph appeared to have been taken from the landing page for a podcast she put out on true crime.

Maya was certain now that this young woman had been targeted by the same killer who had already slain four academics. It would be too much of a coincidence for anything else to have happened to her.

Taking the file, Maya ran over to the interrogation room and hurried in.

"…might as well talk, Ames. You know he wouldn't have any loyalty to you."

"That's where you're wrong," Ames said. "We've fought together, killed together. I know exactly what he would do for me. You think I'll be in here forever? He'll get me out."

Maya could hear the confidence there, and the statement was a confirmation that he'd been in the same military unit as Hanratty, but she had no time to focus on Richard Ames, not now.

"Marco, another potential victim has gone missing," she said. "A TA who runs a podcast where she's talked about the Moonlight Killer."

"Melissa Turner," Ames said, with a slight smile.

Marco pointed at him. "What have you done with her?"

"Me?" Ames raised an eyebrow. "I haven't done anything. But someone will, and soon."

Maya looked over to Marco. "Richard Ames isn't the killer. The real killer is still out there, and every second we waste on Ames, a woman is in danger."

Marco looked conflicted. "And if it *is* Ames? If he's stashed her somewhere? Maybe he's trying to use her as leverage."

That was consistent with what the Moonlight Killer had done with his kidnap victims, but Maya didn't believe that was what was happening here.

"You look into other possibilities if you believe that they're out there," Marco said. "I'm not saying that you shouldn't, but I'm going to stay here with Richard. He's going to tell me where Melissa Turner is."

Richard Ames just smiled.

Maya went back out into the office, feeling frustrated that Marco wasn't listening to her even as she understood why he was so focused on Richard Ames. She headed back to the office trying to think, trying to work out what the killer might have done with Melissa Turner.

The first question was why her body hadn't been found. Why was she missing, not dead and displayed like all the others? Had the killer decided that he needed to display her somewhere special?

What counted as special for him? Maya thought about Evelyn Hart. That had been the one other case where it seemed that he'd gone out of his way to kill a victim in one specific, predetermined spot. Even then, she suspected that a part of it had been because Evelyn's run had taken her close to the spot where the old Moonlight Killer murder had taken place.

But that murder still felt as if it were at the heart of all of this, as if it had been the start for everything that was happening in the town. One murder, leading to four more, potentially five, if Maya couldn't think of something quickly now.

Another question sprang into Maya's mind: *was* that the start of all of this? The killer wasn't following the Moonlight Killer's M.O. now. He was doing something deliberately different. Something designed to stand out.

Was he trying to tell the world that the murder everyone knew the town for *wasn't* the work of the Moonlight Killer? Was this all some twisted way of taking credit? And what if that hadn't been the start of it?

That kill felt too neat, too well planned, for a first kill. If Maya looked, would there be evidence of someone building up to that crime?

Maya started to look through the police records of Miltonberg. In a large city, this wouldn't have worked, because there would simply have been too many murders to work through, but in a place like Miltonberg, the number was more manageable.

Maya started to look through them, started to look for anything with obvious similarities to the kills currently taking place. She tried to narrow them down by M.O., but one stood out immediately because of the location.

There had been a murder on the university campus four years before, in a building on the very fringes of it. Maya quickly pulled up the file for the killing. Instantly, she stopped and stared, because there was a picture of the victim there: Kalinda Green.

She looked so much like Melissa Turner that the resemblance *couldn't* be accidental.

The murder's M.O. wasn't the same as the Moonlight Killer's. Kalinda had been tied and displayed, her throat cut with something that the initial report assumed had been a thin, sharp knife. But, as Maya looked at the pictures in the coroner's report, she couldn't help thinking about the garotte.

Maya hurried back to the interrogation room, knocking on the door until Marco came out.

"I think I know where the killer is taking Melissa Turner," Maya said. She showed Marco the file. "He put Evelyn Hart in the same spot as the Moonlight Killer victim. What if he's taking Melissa to the same place as *this* kill?"

"And what if he isn't?" Marco asked.

"Marco, I'm certain about this. This is where he's heading. Melissa Turner is in danger, and we need to get to the university campus before it's too late."

CHAPTER TWENTY SEVEN

Maya clung on in the car as they skidded around a corner, moving quickly. They had their lights flashing for now, but no siren. If the killer was there at their destination, they couldn't risk alerting him that they were coming. If Melissa Turner was still alive, he would kill her without hesitation and then slip away before they could catch him.

They couldn't risk a woman's life like that, and they couldn't risk letting a killer walk free, either.

They sped forward, heading for the far side of the university campus, where the building in which Kalinda Green had been murdered was located. They were getting closer now, so Maya killed the lights, looking ahead with determination as they sped towards a building that looked old, disused and industrial.

They skidded to a halt in front of the building, the jolt of the sudden stop ricocheting through Maya for a moment before she leaped from the car, looking up at the building.

A sign on the side declared that it was a research facility, but it didn't look as though anyone was currently doing any kind of research in it. The building was dark and quiet, with no sign of anyone moving around in it. The building had an industrial look, with ducting and pipes running along the outside. There were iron steps along the outside, leading to an upper floor.

"This is where a murder took place four years ago?" Marco asked.

Maya nodded. "And, if the killer is revisiting his old scenes, this is where we'll find him."

More importantly, this was where she hoped that they would find Melissa Turner. Maya wanted to believe that they could get to her before it was too late, that they might be able to actually save a life here, rather than just apprehending a killer.

"Does the file show exactly where in the building the first murder took place?" Marco asked.

Maya shook her head. "They just note a lab number and the building. We're going to have to search. We should split up to cover more ground."

She saw Marco hesitate. The look on his face right then wasn't that of a partner, but that of the man she loved and lived with. Maya could see the concern there, the hesitation.

"Are you sure that's a good idea?" he said.

Maya could appreciate the concern, but saving Melissa had to be their number one priority.

"It's our best chance to find Melissa in time. You head around front, I'll take the steps up to the next floor and try to find a way in through there."

"Okay," Marco said. "Just… be careful."

Maya was already heading up the steps, the metal ringing under her feet as she headed up to the next floor of the building. Looking down, she could see Marco moving around the edge of the building, stopping when he came to a spot where a dark van stood as the only evidence that anyone else was in the building at all.

Maya took her eyes from Marco again, continuing up the steps. There were doors at the top, locked, but with a victim potentially in danger, she wasn't about to hold back. She kicked them, hard, her bodyweight behind it the way she'd been trained. The lock gave way to let her into the building.

The interior of the facility was dim, the light barely filtering in from the outside. The corridors held old notices, but the whole place seemed empty, abandoned, as if the university had lost all use for it.

Maya drew her gun, moving smoothly through the space, checking every door she came to. Some were locked, while others opened at her touch, revealing offices and laboratories beyond. Maya cleared each one, knowing that she couldn't risk the possibility of leaving a killer somewhere behind her.

She kept moving, heading deeper into the research building. The twists and turns of the corridors made it hard to keep track of where she was in the building, and even if she did know, that wouldn't help her when she couldn't pin down the exact spot in which the first murder had taken place.

Maya took stairs heading down, checking the corners as she went. She came down onto another floor, then followed a corridor to its end. There was another lab there, larger than the rest, although largely empty now, the equipment long since taken from it.

As Maya opened the door, she stopped and stared.

Melissa Turner was there, tied on a kind of frame, her arms above her head. She appeared to be conscious, although her eyes seemed unfocused, as if she'd been drugged. She was gagged, but she was calling out through that gag, obviously wanting Maya to untie her.

Maya hurried forward, moving to her. She took out the gag first, Melissa's eyes roving around frantically. Then, suddenly, they fixed on a point behind Maya.

"Watch out!"

Maya started to turn. The movement saved her, but even so, a figure slammed into her, sending her gun spinning from her hand, sliding across the laboratory floor. A man shoved her, sending her sprawling in the other direction, but Maya rolled smoothly to her feet.

A man stood in the middle of the room, regarding her with a mixture of anger and curiosity, as if he couldn't quite believe that Maya was in front of him. He was in his forties, with Graying hair and cold green eyes. He was taller than Maya, slender, wearing dark jeans and a t-shirt. The silvery wire of a garrote dangled from one hand. Maya could see the stillness of a killer in his stance, and her heart beat a little faster at the sight of him.

"I guess I should be grateful that you came here, Agent Gray," he said.

"You know who I am," Maya said, trying to keep calm in spite of the potential danger of the situation. "But I don't know your name."

That got another flicker of annoyance. "I guess it doesn't matter now. I'm Shane. Shane Lowell. I was a student here once."

"You're the one who killed the academics?" Maya said. She needed to keep him talking as long as she could. Needed to wait for Marco to get there.

He nodded.

"And the woman attributed to the Moonlight Killer?"

That got another flash of anger, one that made a hint of fear run through Maya. "That was a mistake. I decided that it was a good way to avoid being found."

"But that means that you didn't get the recognition you want?" Maya guessed.

"Do you know how many people I've killed?" Shane asked her.

Maya shook her head. "No."

"No one does," Shane said. He sounded both proud and disappointed. "I've been… too good at what I do. Never the same type of victim, never the same method. Never the same place. Nothing to trace back to me. I travel, you know? For so long, I decided to work outside Miltonberg. I've killed people all around the country. Around the *world*."

"But then you decided that you *did* want the attention?" Maya said. Her eyes were on the spot where her gun lay on the floor. If she could get to it, she could take control of this situation. She started to edge towards it, moving slowly.

"Why should the Moonlight Killer be the only one anyone has heard of?" Shane demanded. "So I decided to find a method that would be consistent. I decided to target the idiots who have given the Moonlight Killer so much attention. I decided to make it clear that nothing in Miltonberg had *ever* been his work."

"So you killed four more people just for the fame?" Maya demanded. Was that his sick reason for all of this? It didn't seem like enough, yet in its own way, the very simplicity of the reason made it into something horrifying, something that no sane person would truly understand.

"It's not just four, though, is it?" Shane said. "When I complete my work here, people will finally connect back to that first kill. Things will come full circle, and people will start to ask why there has been a gap since then. They will realize that there must have been kills in between, but they won't know who, or where. I'll be a terror in the night, someone they can't know, can't place."

"Not if I stop you," Maya said. She was determined now, pushing back the fear she felt. She would take this killer down, whatever it took.

"I can't let you do that," Shane replied. "This is *going* to happen. And… well, maybe there's something to be said for killing the agent who brought down the Moonlight Killer, too. Maybe *that* will be enough to give me my place in history!"

Maya leapt for her gun then. Even as she did it, Shane lashed out, a booted foot catching her in the midsection. For a second, the world exploded in agony, but Maya wasn't going to give in so easily. She lashed out with a kick of her own, catching Shane in the knee, then turned, throwing a palm strike that hit him on the side of the jaw. It staggered him, and Maya saw her chance. She grabbed for her gun again, determined to take control of the situation.

Shane slammed into her, the two of them falling to the ground together. Maya reached out for her weapon, but it was just inches away from her grasp. Shane was behind her then, his weight pressing her into the ground even as Maya tried to twist and escape.

She saw something silvery flash through her line of vision and realized just in time that it had to be the garrote. Maya managed to get her hand in the way, crying out in pain as the wire bit into it, cutting flesh, drawing blood. Shane hauled on the garrote, and Maya felt her hand pulled back tight against her neck. She managed to keep the wire from biting in, managed to keep it from cutting into her arteries, but she could still feel the terrible pressure of it, slowly increasing as Shane continued to pull. Maya tried to buck him off, tried to fight back, but she needed her hands to keep the garrote from cutting into her neck properly. She screamed with the pain of it, and still Shane pulled the weapon tighter.

He was strangling her, and there was nothing Maya could do to stop it.

CHAPTER TWENTY EIGHT

In that moment, Maya knew that she was going to die. It was a realization that brought with it a sense of hopelessness, one that tried to sap her strength, urging her to simply give in to the inevitable, telling her that she could save herself some pain, simply by letting go of the strangling wire cutting into her flesh.

Instead, Maya gripped down tighter on it, ignoring the slickness of her blood on the wire, ignoring the pain as she fought for every second of life. The problem was that she was *only* buying herself seconds with this. Already, Maya could feel her strength waning, could feel the pressure of the garotte building, and darkness starting to close in on her.

"The great Maya Gray," Shane said, above her. "The FBI agent who took down the Moonlight Killer, who solved so many cases claimed as his. It's right, somehow, that I should be the one to kill you. That I finally get to prove that I'm stronger than he ever was."

He hauled on the garrote again, sending a fresh wave of pain through Maya's hand, making the darkness close in further as the pressure on her neck increased.

She thought of Marco in that moment, and the thought of him was enough to bring tears to her eyes when the pain and the prospect of death couldn't. She thought of what it would be like never to see him again. To die here when there were potentially so many years still ahead of them together.

It was enough to make Maya keep fighting, but nothing was working. Nothing could save her, not then. She kept trying to buck free, but she wasn't sure now if her body was even responding the way she wanted. She couldn't feel her limbs now, couldn't even feel the pain anymore.

Distantly, as if coming to her through an ocean's worth of water, Maya heard someone shouting her name. She heard the sound of footsteps, echoing inside her skull, seeming to fill the blackness that was consuming her.

There was a distant, total sense of emptiness, and then… then there was impact. An impact that seemed to be everywhere, sending a sudden, wrenching jolt of pain through Maya.

In an instant, she could breathe again. Maya gasped for air, pain and light and sound flooding back to her.

She saw Marco then, struggling with Shane Lowell. The two men were trading punches, Marco throwing an uppercut at Shane, Shane slamming a hook into Marco's ribs. Maya could see Marco's gun on the floor. It took her a second to realize that he must have dropped it during the struggle.

Why hadn't he used it the moment he came into the room? Maya tried to think and realized that he must not have had a clear shot when Shane had been pressed so close to Maya trying to kill her. He'd taken the only option available to him and tackled the killer, which now left the two of them fighting hand to hand, lashing out with fists, knees and elbows.

For a second or two, all Maya could do was lie there and watch the battle between the two men, trying to get air into her lungs, slowly feeling the strength come back into her limbs. She saw Shane try to claw at Marco's eyes, saw Marco turn his head aside, slamming a cross into Shane's jaw that made him stumble. Marco closed the distance, following up with short punches to Shane's body.

Shane responded with a tackle that caught Marco by surprise, taking the two of them to the floor. Shane came up on top, swinging punches. Marco rolled him for a second, but then Shane caught him with a kick that slammed upwards into his jaw. Maya winced at the impact, especially as Marco reeled from it, falling from Shane for a second.

It was all the killer needed to get up, scrambling for the spot where Marco's gun lay on the floor. Terror filled Maya in that moment, for Marco, for herself, for Melissa Turner.

Maya still felt half unconscious from being strangled, but she knew that she had no time to hesitate. Ignoring the way her body protested, she pushed to her knees, and then threw herself forward, snagging Shane's ankle as he closed in on the gun. Maya turned it into a low takedown, dragging Shane to the floor again, holding on with all her remaining strength as Shane continued to reach for the gun.

Maya was on top of him then, her arm wrapping around his neck. She could feel agony in the palm of her left hand where it had intercepted the garotte, but Maya didn't care right then. She was totally focused on Shane, on stopping the threat he represented. She locked up the choke, squeezing with all the strength she had left.

Still, it wasn't enough. Somehow, Shane managed to get his hands and feet under him, bringing himself to an awkward crouch, then standing with Maya clinging to his back like a backpack. She knew that she ought to bail out of the choke then, to move off Shane's back and take him back down, but she was a fraction of a second too late.

He threw himself backward, his weight slamming into Maya as they both hit the floor. Maya found herself caught between the hammer of the falling killer and the anvil of the lab's floor, the impact of the slam enough to make her see stars, losing her grip on Shane.

He was up in an instant, lunging for the gun once more. Maya saw Marco move to intercept him, the two of them fighting over the gun, trying to gain control of it. Maya's heart was in her mouth, knowing that the next few moments might mean the difference between life and death for everyone in the room.

Maya looked around, trying to find a way to help. She was still stunned, her vision swimming, her limbs barely responding. She spotted her own weapon, still there where it had fallen on the floor.

Maya crawled for it because she didn't have the strength to stand and lunge for it. Her body complained with every movement, the weapon seeming so close, yet still an eternity away.

She saw Shane slam his head into Marco's face once, then again. It was enough to make Marco fall back, and then Shane was standing over him, the pistol cradled in his hands, ready to fire.

Maya gathered the last of her strength, flinging herself forward, her hand grasping for the grip of her weapon. She rolled onto her back, bringing it to bear, trying to ignore the way the room seemed to swim around her with the movement. She wasn't sure that she could hit anything like this, wasn't sure that she could actually do what was required in that moment.

"Shane, stop, or I'll shoot!" she called out, hoping that the threat would be enough, hoping that at the very least, it would buy some time for her to be able to see straight again.

Shane just stood there over Marco, gun rising to point straight at his head. Maya felt a surge of fear flood through her, and she knew that there was no more time to wait. She pulled the trigger, the sound of the shot echoing in her ears as she fired.

She saw Shane stagger as the shot hit him in the shoulder, the weapon he held falling from his hands.

That gave Marco an opportunity to move in on Shane, grabbing him and bearing him to the ground, holding him in place even while he cried out in pain.

Maya moved over to help him, wrenching Shane's arms behind his back in spite of his struggles. With the two of them working together, there was no way for him to resist. Maya got out her handcuff, clicking them into place on his wrists.

She limped over to Melissa, cutting her down from where she'd been tied. The young woman collapsed into her arms.

"It's all right," Maya said. "It's over. It's done."

CHAPTER TWENTY NINE

Of course, it wasn't done.

"Swift wants to talk to you in her office," Marco said. "I guess she wants to talk about the report for the Miltonberg murders."

The aftermath of taking down a killer like Shane Lowell meant plenty more work back at the FBI headquarters. It meant putting together reports, interrogating their perpetrator, making sure that they had enough to convict him. It also meant Maya dealing with her new boss.

"All right, I'll head up," Maya said.

"Do you want me to come with you?" Marco asked.

Maya smiled over at him. "I always want you with me. But for this, I should probably do it alone."

She leaned in to kiss him, not caring where they were, or that the deputy director was waiting for her.

"I love you," Marco whispered, as they parted.

"I love you too," Maya said. She reached up to touch his face, then winced and pulled her bandaged hand back.

"Your hand's still hurting?" Marco asked.

Maya nodded. It was only to be expected, though. The doctors had stitched up her hand where the wire garrote had cut into it, but it had only been a couple of days since they'd captured Shane and it was a long way from fully healed. It would be one more scar to add to the others that dotted Maya's body.

"It will be fine," she assured him. "Now, I should probably head up to see Swift."

She hurried over to the elevator, riding up towards the top of the building. She strode over to Deputy Director Swift's office. The door was open, and the deputy director waved her inside. Maya stood in front of her desk until Swift made a small gesture for her to sit down without saying anything. Her frequent annoyance with Maya wasn't there, though. If anything, she looked happy with her. That was such a rare sight that Maya took a moment to savor it.

"I've been reading through your report," Swift said. "Well done on stopping this one. If this is correct, we're looking at a serial killer who might have as many old murders to his name as the Moonlight Killer."

"It might be difficult to identify exactly which ones," Maya said. "He seems to have varied his M.O. deliberately to keep us from working out which kills are his. Although, since he seems to want the attention now, it may be possible to leverage that to get him to give us a full list."

"Possibly," Swift said. "Although I dislike having to rely on the word of a psychopath like that. They are unreliable at best." She paused for a moment. "I should say that I'm talking to the local DA about the possibility of charges against Lisa Franklin for holding back information about one of those who helped Francis Hanratty to escape."

Maya wasn't entirely surprised that Swift had gone after the reporter for that. The deputy director wanted the Moonlight Killer behind bars almost more than Maya did, so she wouldn't react well to anyone helping him by holding back information on his followers.

"How is the hunt for Hanratty going?" Maya asked. She couldn't help herself. Even though she knew that Swift wanted to keep her on the fringes of that investigation, she was determined to play a part in it. She wanted to make sure that her sister, and the other women who he had kidnapped, would be safe. The only way to do that was to put him back behind bars.

"That is a part of why I called you up here," Swift said. She steepled her fingers, giving Maya a level look. "You did well, taking Richard Ames into custody. He'll pay for his part in helping Hanratty to escape, but now, he isn't talking."

That made a kind of sense.

"He didn't say much back in Miltonberg, either," Maya said. "He also claims that he doesn't know anything about where Hanratty is right now, for 'operational security'."

"A worrying phrase," Swift said, her eyes narrowing slightly. "It implies that there is some bigger plan in play here than simply keeping a killer out of prison."

That was consistent with what Maya had seen of Hanratty in some ways. He was good at planning, ferociously intelligent, dangerously driven. He'd shown how easily he could manipulate others into doing what he wanted and, more recently, it seemed that he'd acquired some truly fanatical followers. Maya didn't want to think about what a serial killer with an almost cult-like following could achieve.

"There will be some plan," Maya agreed, "although I'm not sure about it being some huge team effort. The one thing that seems to be consistent about Hanratty is that, for him, everything is *about* him. He kills alone. He doesn't like competition."

"Maybe he's changing," Swift replied.

Change was the thing he stopped in other people. Was it possible that Francis Hanratty had changed?

"In any case, it doesn't matter," Swift said. "What matters is that Richard Ames is refusing to talk to anyone but you."

That caught Maya a little by surprise. "He wasn't prepared to talk to me back in Miltonberg."

She saw Swift shrug. "Well, maybe a couple of days in a federal holding cell have given him time to think about what the rest of his life is going to be like."

"You think he wants to make a deal?" Maya asked.

Swift nodded. "If so, if he can give us Hanratty, we're prepared to offer him a deal on his role in the escape."

"And if he wants more than that?" Maya asked.

Swift sat there, considering it for several seconds. "Hanratty is the priority. Make any promise you need to. Do what you need to do. Just get me a location for him."

It was easy to forget, sometimes, that Swift was at least as driven to catch Francis Hanratty as Maya was.

"I'll talk to him," Maya promised.

"He's already waiting for you in an interrogation room."

It seemed that Swift had known how this would turn out from the moment Maya had walked into the room. Maya stood and headed for the door.

"And Gray… if you get the information, this time, you're in on the raid to take Hanratty down. I won't try to keep you out."

That was the biggest concession that Swift could offer her. The last time she'd gone after the Moonlight Killer, Maya had had to do it alone, both because she hadn't trusted Hanratty not to run if he saw the FBI coming, and because she'd thought that Swift might try to keep her out of the last phase of the hunt for him. This time, it seemed that Swift was willing to work with her.

Maya made her way down to the interrogation room, where Richard Ames was waiting with his lawyer: a pale, sandy-haired young man who looked like he was fresh out of law school. He looked more nervous than Ames did as Maya walked in, taking a seat opposite the pair at the metal table that dominated the room.

"You wanted to see me?" Maya asked.

The lawyer spoke before Ames could. "I'm Robert McCallum, representing Mr. Ames. He has some information that he is willing to provide to the FBI."

"I'm all ears," Maya said, looking straight at Ames, not at his lawyer, trying to gauge what he was doing. He didn't seem as nervous as he had the last time she'd interrogated him. Maybe that was because of the prospect of getting out of here.

"Before he says anything, my client wants immunity and protection," the lawyer said.

"The last time I spoke to your client, he told me that he didn't know the one thing I wanted to know," Maya said. "Remember, Richard? You said that you didn't know where the Moonlight Killer was, so that you couldn't be made to tell anyone."

"I don't know where he is," Ames said.

Maya stood up with a shrug. "Then we have nothing to talk about here."

She headed for the door.

"I know where he's *going* to be, though," Ames said.

Maya paused, but didn't turn around. "I'm listening."

"Immunity," the lawyer said.

Maya paused. "I'm authorized to offer immunity for any charges relating to Hanratty's escape from custody."

"That's not enough," the lawyer said.

"Given that we don't have evidence of any other crimes, what else does he need immunity for?" Maya asked. "Are you about to admit to something we don't know about, Richard?"

"What about protection?" Ames said.

Maya looked back at him. "Are you looking for witness relocation? Because we can talk about that, but we both know that the best protection for you is if Hanratty is in prison."

She could see the uncertainty there on Ames's face. "Think about it, Richard. Francis Hanratty does not forgive people who fail him. He kills them. He's shown that he can get to people inside prisons. Do you want to sit in one, knowing that, any day, he might come and kill you?"

She watched Richard Ames, watching the calculation on his face as he tried to make a decision. Watching him trying to decide what his best chance of survival was. Finally, he looked down, defeated.

"All right," he said. "He's gathering a group of us together, out in the woods for some big plan of his. I can tell you where."

"And you've just had a sudden change of heart on all of this?" Maya said, not quite trusting Ames' words.

He looked her straight in the eyes. "You said it yourself: he'll kill me now. I know better than anyone else just how dangerous he is. If I don't give you the meeting, then I'm a dead man."

"When is it?" Maya demanded.

Ames laughed. "When do you think? Under the full moon."

Maya felt her heart beating faster at that, and at the thought that she would soon have a location for both the Moonlight Killer and his little coterie of followers. With that information, it would be possible to plan an ambush that might take down, not just Francis Hanratty, but his entire organization.

Maya was determined not to waste that chance. She would go to Swift, they would plan this ambush together, and then… she would take down the Moonlight Killer again. She would throw him in a hole so deep that he would *never* see the light of day again.

CHAPTER THIRTY

"Teams, check in."

Maya looked over at Swift as the deputy director spoke into her radio. Swift looked uncharacteristically nervous. Maya was used to her being in complete control, never seeming less than confident.

They were currently parked up off a forest track, along with an FBI tactical team. Maya knew from the planning for all of this that more teams were moving through the forest from different directions, converging on the spot where the meeting of the Moonlight Killer's followers was due to take place.

Marco was there by Maya's side. Both he and Maya were in full tactical gear, including a tactical vest, helmet and night vision goggles. Maya had a night vision scope on her rifle, while Marco had again decided to favor a shotgun. Maya's hand was stitched and bandaged. She hoped that the pain wouldn't distract her if she needed to take a shot.

"Team one, in position."

"Team two, in position."

"Team three, in position."

"Aerial recon team, awaiting instructions."

Swift moved over to Maya. To Maya's surprise, the deputy director seemed to be including her in the planning for this raid. Maya couldn't tell if it was so that she could spread the blame if things went wrong, or because she respected Maya's expertise when it came to the Moonlight Killer.

"Everyone's in place. We'll send drones up to scout."

"That might be a bad idea," Maya replied. "We know that Hanratty is paranoid about security, and we know that he's scanned for law enforcement channels before. If he spots a feed from a drone, it might be enough to spook him."

"So, what do you recommend?" Swift asked. "Going in blind? Keeping radio silence?"

Maya nodded. “At least until we get eyes on our suspects. We move in carefully, we make sure that this isn’t just one more trap laid by Hanratty. Then we move.”

“So why bring the ARUs at all?” Swift asked. “I even have a chopper standing by.”

"Because if he runs, I want to know where he's going,” Maya replied. “We make the initial approach without them, but the moment this starts to get hot, we use them for backup.”

She heard Swift sigh. “All right. With anyone else, I would say you were being too cautious, but we’ve lost people to his tricks before. I’ll order radio silence, then we’re going to move in.”

“You’re coming with us, ma’am?” Marco asked. “Not staying here at the command post?”

Swift smiled in the moonlight. “Do you really think I’m going to miss out on the chance to see Francis Hanratty’s face when we take him down? Get ready to move out. Gray, you take point!”

Maya nodded. She’d insisted on that part. She knew how Hanratty’s mind worked by now, knew his penchant for traps. She wanted to be the one checking the route for danger, rather than following a tactical team blindly, hoping that they’d cleared anything Hanratty put in their path.

She crept through the forest. The moonlight filtered through the trees, the bright glow of the full moon giving Maya just enough light to see by as she padded forward, heading for the map reference Richard Ames had provided. She moved in silence, taking in the sounds of the forest: the movement of small animals and the hoot of an owl.

Ahead, she could see lights. Maya moved towards them carefully, looking around to check that Marco and the others were in step with her. Marco was right there at her shoulder. Swift was behind him, the tactical team keeping close to her, obviously knowing how bad it would be if something happened to the deputy director.

Maya caught a glimpse of something shining silver in the moonlight. She held a hand up to halt the others, then crouched, finding the tripwire. Following it along, she found the claymore mine it was attached to. It took her another few seconds to disarm it before continuing to move. She just had to hope that the other tactical teams would be able to avoid any similar devices.

She approached the lights cautiously, crouching in the trees, not wanting to give away her position. She saw that there, in a clearing, was a cabin that was far too much like the one where Hanratty had built a bunker to hold his victims. The clearing held barrels and a couple of low, fenced off areas. There were people gathered around, men and women, most of them dressed in dark clothes, most of them armed. There had to be at least thirty of them.

Were these the Moonlight Killer's followers? Were these the people who had helped to get him out of prison, who had kidnapped for him, killed for him?

Maya had her answer as the door to the cabin opened and there, framed in the light from the cabin, was Francis Hanratty.

He was in is forties, muscular and athletic, his hair cropped short, his features good looking but ultimately unmemorable. He walked with the slightest of limps, a memento of when Maya had shot him the first time she'd caught him. He was dressed all in black.

He addressed the waiting crowd from the doorway of the cabin, his voice warm in the way that said he was making an effort to be charming.

"My friends, welcome. You are the trusted few, the ones who are worthy. The ones who have a part in the culmination of my plan. Again and again, there have been those who have begged me for details of it. Who have tried to see some hidden truth behind what I've been saying to them? Now, you're all here. Everything has been leading to this moment."

He paused for effect, and Maya tried to still her breathing. Hanratty was right, everything *had* been leading to this moment. To the moment when she would stop him.

Maya had him in her sights. It would be so easy to end this, once and for all. She couldn't do that, though. She was an FBI agent. She had to uphold the law. She kept waiting, and Hanratty kept talking.

"This is your moment. This is the reason I brought you here... because the FBI are here. Aren't you, Agent Gray?"

He called that out into the night and Maya cursed, realizing that once again, he'd found a way to set her up. He must have instructed Richard Ames to leak the time and place of this meet-up, all as a way to lure Maya in. He'd set a trap for her.

And not just for her, if the looks on the faces of his followers there were anything to go by.

Yet he'd made one mistake. For the trap to work, he'd had to use himself as bait. He must have known that Maya wouldn't make a move unless she saw him. Now, though... now he was there, and that meant that there was still a chance to end this.

"Go!" Maya called out to the others, and she saw Swift grabbing for her radio.

"All teams, green light! Go!"

The FBI tactical teams surged from the trees, and in under a second, the whole clearing erupted into chaos. Figures dove for cover among the barrels and the fences, gunfire erupting all around. Maya's eyes were on Hanratty as she burst from the clearing, but she had to duck down to avoid a burst of fire coming from ahead. Maya fired back, not knowing if she hit anything, and kept moving.

That second of delay cost her dearly. She saw that Hanratty had a weapon raised, a rifle of his own, and he seemed to smile as he took aim. It took her a fraction of a second to realize that he wasn't aiming at her.

"Down!" Maya shouted, throwing herself at Marco as the shot came. She slammed into him, knocking him to the side, but even as she did so, she saw blood burst from his side, heard his grunt of pain as the bullet struck him. "Marco, no! Medic!"

She dragged him back towards the trees while the gun battle raged around her. Swift was there, along with the tag-team's medic. Marco was groaning in pain, his features pale with it. Maya didn't know what the shot had struck or how bad it was. There was no way of telling in the moonlight.

"We've got him," Swift said. "Make sure that Hanratty doesn't get away."

"Go, Maya!" Marco said, his voice weak. "Get that bastard!"

Maya needed no further urging. She sprinted forward. She could see Hanratty disappearing into the trees, using the battle between the FBI and his followers for cover as he slipped away.

Maya wasn't going to allow him to get away. Not after everything he'd done. Not after what he'd *just* done. He was going to pay.

Maya hurried into the trees, following in his footsteps, trusting that the tactical teams could take down the others in the clearing. Maya didn't care about the others right then, only about Hanratty.

"This way, dear Maya," he called out.

He was all but invisible in the trees, now. He was ahead of her somewhere, taunting her, calling her on. The gunfire and the sounds of battle confused the noises around them, while the trees seemed to distort the sounds, making it hard to pin down his location.

"Did you really think that it would be that easy to catch me?" he called out, his location different now, away to her left instead. He was playing cat and mouse with her, and the worst part was that Maya wasn't sure which one she was. She felt a thread of fear invade the anger that filled her, but she pushed it aside.

She moved silently now, stalking him, knowing that this was a deadly killer, but that she was every bit as dangerous here and now. She could feel cold determination settling in her. If Francis Hanratty came into view right then, she would have fired without a second thought.

"All those people back there thought that I was going to lead them," Hanratty said. "They thought that I had some grand vision for them to follow. It only shows how foolish people can be. Do you know what my big plan was, Maya? What my goal is?"

Maya didn't answer. She kept moving, kept stalking him, her eyes scanning the trees.

"All of this was about the chance to stalk one person, one perfect victim who has come so far," Hanratty said.

Maya whirled, seeking out that voice. She didn't fire, but only because discipline kept her from wasting the ammunition. She started towards the voice. It was close now.

"It was about you."

Those words were whispered practically in Maya's ear, and her adrenaline spiked. She had a moment to realize that he'd tricked her, that he was using his so-called followers to distract the rest of the FBI teams, that he'd lured her away by hurting Marco, that he had her alone now.

Then there was a rope going around her neck, dragging her back.

CHAPTER THIRTY ONE

Maya let go of her grip on her rifle as the Moonlight Killer dragged her back, letting it fall uselessly on the strap that held it. At such close range, there was no way of bringing it to bear.

She didn't grab for the rope around her neck. She knew that Francis Hanratty didn't use the same kind of cutting wire garotte that Shane Lowell had used. She also knew that there was no point trying to wrench Hanratty's grip free. She knew how strong he was.

Her only option was to attack.

Maya reached down to her belt, pulling out a knife. She twisted into Hanratty, stabbing into his leg, eliciting a hiss of pain. Hanratty leg go of his grip on the rope. Maya guessed that it wasn't just down to the pain, that it had more to do with her foe wanting to be able to defend against any other attacks from the knife.

Hanratty's hands clamped onto Maya's arm. He slammed a knee up into her stomach, the impact doubling Maya over. He smashed her hand into the nearest tree, the pain of it making Maya's fingers open reflexively. The knife tumbled to the forest floor.

Maya kicked out, using Hanratty as a surface to push back from as much as trying to simply hurt him. She wanted enough room to bring another weapon to bear, wanted the space to finish this rather than fighting hand to hand.

Maya managed to break Hanratty's grip, falling back to the forest floor away from him, scrambling to bring up her rifle. He was already moving back into the trees as she fired, the sound of the short burst of fire filling the air.

He was slipping away, so Maya had to follow, hunting him through the dark. She saw another glimpse of movement and fired, splintering the tree that he was behind. Shots came back through the dark. It seemed that Hanratty had switched back to his own rifle, firing carefully.

Maya could feel her adrenaline pumping. She knew that she had to be careful. Hanratty had failed to kill her up close, but that didn't mean that she was safe. If anything, it meant that he would switch to other methods now, and this man was a trained killer, one used to violence.

Maya couldn't just charge out after him. She had to take a circling path through the trees, moving from cover to cover, shots coming as she moved from spot to spot. Maya fired back, as much to make Hanratty duck into his own cover as because she thought that it would hit him. That was the only way she could buy enough time to keep moving closer to him, to keep stalking forward towards him.

Maya caught more glimpses of Hanratty as he moved from cover to cover. He moved quickly, with no rhythm to the movements that Maya might figure out in order to guess when he might make his next move. Each time Maya fired, she was a fraction of a second too late, so that he was already behind the next tree before Maya could get a bead on him.

He was moving further away from Maya, limping where she'd stabbed him, trailing blood, drawing her deeper into the forest. Further away from the tactical teams who might help her. Maya knew that he was trying to lure her forward to her doom, but right then, Maya didn't care. This was the man who had kidnapped her sister, who had shot Marco. She would follow him to the ends of the earth if she had to.

She kept moving, kept firing. She reloaded once and kept going, dodging as best she could while Hanratty fired back, the two of them trading bullets like tennis players hitting a ball back and forth. How much more ammunition would Hanratty have? How long would he be able to keep this up?

Almost as if in answer to her thought, Hanratty stopped firing, silence reigning over the forest once more.

Did that mean that he was out? Did it mean that he was just reloading? As the silence continued, Maya feared that he might be trying to escape silently into the night, living to fight another day.

Or maybe she'd hit him with one of her shots and he was already down. Maybe the man who had shot Marco and kidnapped Maya's sister was lying dead on the forest floor somewhere.

Either way, Maya had no choice other than to move forward. She did it carefully, keeping off the path, her weapon sweeping left and right as her eyes scanned the shadows of the forest. She had to work by moonlight, not daring to turn on a flashlight and give away her position. She hunted Francis Hanratty through the dark, listening for any crack of branches underfoot, looking for any shapes that didn't fit the surrounding foliage.

She was almost at the spot where she thought Hanratty might be hiding when she heard movement away to her left. Maya threw herself into cover behind a fallen tree, instinct propelling her.

She was just in time as shots came over her head, striking the trees behind her. Maya had to lie flat as another burst of fire came. She didn't dare to raise her head, because that would only present a target. Instead, she had to lift her weapon and fire blind, trying to take back some of the initiative.

She looked around, trying to find a way to get back into the trees, but the fallen log was in the middle of a clear area, the full moon shining down on it. If Maya rose to run, she would be an easy target.

All she could do was lie there, continuing to fire back as Francis Hanratty kept her pinned in place, just trying to keep him at bay for long enough that backup might arrive.

Then her rifle clicked empty, the sound surprisingly loud, even against the backdrop of the gunfire. Maya cursed and tossed the weapon aside, drawing her pistol.

"Looks like this is how it ends for you, Maya," Hanratty said. "I might not get to strangle you, but at least you'll die under the full moon."

Maya heard the crunch of his boots as he started to move forward. She could picture him advancing on her, weapon ready. She knew that if she just lay there, he would be on top of her in seconds and she would die.

There was only one chance, but that was almost as likely to get her killed as staying there would. Maya thought of Marco then, potentially bleeding out while a medic tried to help him. She thought of her sister, Megan, hiding at their aunt's house, as if that would stop a serial killer. She thought of all the people Francis Hanratty had hurt, had killed, all the people he might *still* kill.

Anger boiled through Maya, and she flung herself from her cover. She heard the sound of gunfire as Hanratty tried to finish her, and Maya felt the impact of something in her side. She was firing too, and it didn't matter whether she missed or hit, so long as she kept up the pressure.

She slammed into him, hitting him with a headbutt, then an elbow strike. Maya wrenched the gun from his hands, flinging it away. He got both hands to her weapon arm, holding on so that Maya wouldn't be able to bring her gun to bear. She kept hitting him, kept lashing out, not wanting to give him a chance to recover. Hanratty was stronger than her, but all his strength was focused on preventing Maya from shooting him.

That meant that her other arm was free to start raining blows on him, staggering him back, making it easy to trip him. Maya ignored the pain in her side as she did so, ignored the damage that Hanratty might already have done. They hit the floor together, and Hanratty wrenched Maya's arm, the gun dropping from her hand. He came up on top, his hands questing for her throat now.

"Maybe I get to strangle you after all."

Maya struggled, twisting to get her legs between them, but Hanratty kept squeezing. Maya twisted underneath him, her legs going up to wrap up his arms. She grabbed one of them, driving her hips in, hyperextending the elbow joint. She heard a cry of pain from Hanratty as his elbow popped, but Maya didn't hesitate. She kicked away from him, rolling to her feet, grabbing her pistol and raising it.

Hanratty was on his back, cradling his arm and staring up at Maya with obvious hatred.

"Do it," he said. "Finish this."

Maya could feel the adrenaline pumping through her veins as she stood there over him, the weapon leveled at his body now. It would have been so easy to simply pull the trigger in that moment. So easy to put an end to the evil of a man who had terrorized so many, who might have killed Marco. It took an effort of will for Maya not to fire.

"Do it," Hanratty said. "You know a prison won't hold me. You know I'll still have people on the outside. You will *never* be safe."

Maya took a step back, making sure that he wasn't close enough to grab for her. She reached for her radio, determined to call this in, determined to get back up there to make sure that Francis Hanratty was contained.

"You're going to rot in prison," Maya said. "I think you played all your cards this time, and there's nothing left for you except to try to get me to kill you."

Hanratty howled with anger and pain, his hand suddenly going to the small of his back. Maya had enough time to see a small pistol in his hand, rising towards her in the moonlight.

Then the sound of a shot rang out, and Hanratty slumped back to the forest floor.

Maya looked around and saw the source of the shot. Marco was there, leaning on Swift, his weapon unsteady now in his hand. His side was bandaged, but Maya could see blood seeping through the bandages.

She ran to Hanratty, kicking the gun from his hand. She needn't have bothered. His eyes were wide, empty and staring, looking up sightlessly in death at the full moon above, the way so many of his victims had.

The Moonlight Killer was dead. It was finally over.

CHAPTER THIRTY TWO

Maya tried not to show too much pain as she and Marco sat in Swift's office, waiting for the deputy director to arrive.

They both had bandages and new scars under their suits, thanks to Francis Hanratty. In theory, they should both have been at home, recuperating from their stays at the hospital in the wake of the raid on Hanratty's meeting of his followers. Neither of them had been able to stay away.

"Wishing you were at home?" Marco asked her.

Maya smiled. "Yes, but I need to be here."

"How are your injuries doing?"

"I should be asking you that question," Maya said. Marco was the one who had been hurt worse. Marco was the one who had trekked through a forest towards the sound of gunfire even after he'd been shot, knowing that Maya was in danger.

Without him, Maya would be dead.

"I'm fine," Marco assured her.

"You're a terrible liar."

"It's just one of the things you love about me."

Maya nodded. "True."

They were interrupted by Swift entering her office. Maya made to stand, but the deputy director waved the attempt away. Maya was grateful for that. Moving still hurt.

"Agents, thank you for coming in. I thought you would want to hear what's been going on in your absence, and after all you've done, I think you deserve to be kept in the loop."

From Swift, that was a concession after so long trying to keep Maya on the outside.

"Have there been developments?" Maya asked.

"You won't be facing a review over the death of Francis Hanratty," Swift said, looking at Marco. "Given the circumstances, it's obvious that he posed an immediate threat to life. I wanted to tell you that right away."

Maya was relieved by that. She hadn't believed that Marco had anything to worry about, but it was good to have it confirmed.

"I also wanted to say that we've been working to wrap up the network Hanratty built," Swift said. "The cabin held records for many of them, and some of those people we caught there have been able to tell us about others. We should be able to make quick progress."

"Will you need us for that, ma'am?" Maya asked.

"I appreciate the enthusiasm, Gray, but you and Spinelli need to focus on healing up properly. There will be plenty more work for you both once you're well."

That was both a relief and a disappointment. A relief, because Maya wasn't sure that she was physically up to chasing down criminals right then. A disappointment, because she wanted to make sure that all of the Moonlight Killer's influence was rooted out. She didn't want any hint of it left behind.

"So, what will we be doing next?" Marco asked.

Swift looked at them both. "It's obvious that the pair of you are more effective as partners than separately. I'm inclined to assign you to the field office that Gray has been running, Spinnelli, to see how much of a difference the two of you can make there."

Maya looked over to Marco. Would he want to give up working undercover to take down organized crime in order to work alongside Maya? Would he be willing to go from working out of the FBI HQ to working at a field office?

"That sounds perfect," Marco said.

Maya felt a wave of relief flooding through her at the sound of that.

"All right," Swift said. "That will be all for now. I'll let you know if anything changes. For now, go home, get some rest."

Maya stood, wincing slightly at the movement. She and Marco left the office, heading back towards the elevator.

"It's a good job that was short," Marco said as they left. "If Megan's coming over for dinner, we'll need to get back."

Maya smiled at the thought of her sister being able to come out of hiding at their aunt's place, at the fact that the threat to her family was over now. She put a hand on Marco's arm.

"You're really okay giving up all this to come work at a field office?"

"Anywhere, to be with you," Marco said. "Besides, we make a good team."

They did, and Maya was already thinking about all the cases that the two of them could work together. She wasn't going to let herself get stuck in the office again. She was determined to get out in the field, to make a difference.

"You know," Maya said. "There's still *one* case somewhere wrongly attributed to the Moonlight Killer. One killer out there somewhere who has gotten away with murder because we all think it was Hanratty."

Marco took her by the shoulders, kissing her deeply. It was a surprise, but Maya leaned into it.

"What was that for?" she asked, as they broke apart.

"Because I love you."

"And also…"

"And also to distract you," Marco admitted. "You're in no condition to go running off after killers yet."

"But I will be," Maya said. "*We* will be."

"And when we are, I'm sure there will be plenty of killers out there. For now, though, maybe we just take some time to heal."

Maya knew that Marco had a point. There would always be more killers out there. It wasn't as if taking down the Moonlight Killer would stop that. When she and Marco went back to work, there would be plenty of cases waiting for them.

For now, though, they had time to rest, and they had each other. Serial killers could wait.

NOW AVAILABLE!

BEHIND HER LIES
(An Elise Close Psychological Thriller—Book One)

"I binge read this book. It hooked me in and didn't stop till the last few pages… I look forward to reading more!"
—Reader review for Found You

Celebrity therapist Elise Close is no stranger to families with skeletons in their closets.

But when she crosses the threshold into the Nolan household on Boston's exclusive Beacon Hill, she may be entering a crypt of secrets and lies.

Hired to treat their son's sudden engagement-induced turmoil, Elise discovers a psychopathic person and cunning agenda that could ruin the family's legacy.

But with sleepless nights and overmedication, distinguishing friend from foe becomes a perilous game. Can Elise maintain her grasp on reality long enough to protect a legacy?

Or will she be undone by ghosts of her own making?

BEHIND HER LIES is the first book in a highly anticipated new psychological suspense series by critically-acclaimed and #1 bestselling mystery and suspense author Molly Black, whose books have received over 2,000 five-star reviews and ratings.

Future books in the series are also available!

"Molly Black has written a taut thriller that will keep you on the edge of your seat… I absolutely loved this book and can't wait to read the next book in the series!"

—Reader review for Girl One: Murder

"I loved this book! Fast-paced plot, great characters and interesting insights into investigating cold cases. I can't wait to read the next book!"
—Reader review for Girl One: Murder

"Very good book… You will feel like you are right there looking for the kidnapper! I know I will be reading more in this series!"
—Reader review for Girl One: Murder

"This is a very well written book and holds your interest from page 1… Definitely looking forward to reading the next one in the series, and hopefully others as well!"
—Reader review for Girl One: Murder

"Wow, I cannot wait for the next in this series. Starts with a bang and just keeps going."
—Reader review for Girl One: Murder

"Well written book with a great plot, one that will keep you up at night. A page turner!"
—Reader review for Girl One: Murder

"A great suspense that keeps you reading… can't wait for the next in this series!"
—Reader review for Found You

"Sooo soo good! There are a few unforeseen twists… I binge read this like I binge watch Netflix. It just sucks you in."
—Reader review for Found You

Molly Black

Bestselling author Molly Black is author of the MAYA GRAY FBI suspense thriller series, comprising eleven books; of the RYLIE WOLF FBI suspense thriller series, comprising six books; of the TAYLOR SAGE FBI suspense thriller series, comprising eight books; of the KATIE WINTER FBI suspense thriller series, comprising eleven books (and counting); of the RUBY HUNTER FBI suspense thriller series, comprising five books (and counting); of the CAITLIN DARE FBI suspense thriller series, comprising six books (and counting); of the REESE LINK mystery series, comprising six books (and counting); of the CLAIRE KING FBI suspense thriller series, comprising seven books (and counting); of the PIPER WOODS mystery series, comprising five books (and counting); of the GRACE FORD mystery series, comprising seven books (and counting); of the CASEY BOLT mystery series, comprising five books (and counting); of the JADE SAVAGE mystery series, comprising five books (and counting); of the TESSA FLINT mystery series, comprising five books (and counting); of the CLARA PIKE FBI thriller series, comprising five books (and counting); and of the ELISE CLOSE psychological thriller series, comprising five books (and counting).

An avid reader and lifelong fan of the mystery and thriller genres, Molly loves to hear from you, so please feel free to visit www.mollyblackauthor.com to learn more and stay in touch.

BOOKS BY MOLLY BLACK

ELISE CLOSE MYSTERY SERIES

BEHIND HER LIES (Book #1)
BEHIND HER SMILE (Book #2)
BEHIND HER SECRETS (Book #3)
BEHIND HER GATES (Book #4)
BEHIND LOCKED DOORS (Book #5)

CASEY BOLT MYSTERY SERIES

BROKEN (Book #1)
FLAWED (Book #2)
BLEMISHED (Book #3)
DAMAGED (Book #4)
TWISTED (Book #5)

GRACE FORD MYSTERY SERIES

NEARLY MINE (Book #1)
NEARLY SAFE (Book #2)
NEARLY FREE (Book #3)
NEARLY GONE (Book #4)
NEARLY HIS (Book #5)

CLAIRE KING MYSTERY SERIES

ONCE HE SEES (Book #1)
ONCE HE LONGS (Book #2)
ONCE HE TAKES (Book #3)
ONCE HE FEELS (Book #4)
ONCE HE KNOWS (Book #5)

MAYA GRAY MYSTERY SERIES

GIRL ONE: MURDER (Book #1)
GIRL TWO: TAKEN (Book #2)
GIRL THREE: TRAPPED (Book #3)

GIRL FOUR: LURED (Book #4)
GIRL FIVE: BOUND (Book #5)
GIRL SIX: FORSAKEN (Book #6)
GIRL SEVEN: CRAVED (Book #7)
GIRL EIGHT: HUNTED (Book #8)
GIRL NINE: GONE (Book #9)

RYLIE WOLF FBI SUSPENSE THRILLER
FOUND YOU (Book #1)
CAUGHT YOU (Book #2)
SEE YOU (Book #3)
WANT YOU (Book #4)
TAKE YOU (Book #5)
DARE YOU (Book #6)

TAYLOR SAGE FBI SUSPENSE THRILLER
DON'T LOOK (Book #1)
DON'T BREATHE (Book #2)
DON'T RUN (Book #3)
DON'T FLINCH (Book #4)
DON'T REMEMBER (Book #5)
DON'T TELL (Book #6)

KATIE WINTER FBI SUSPENSE THRILLER
SAVE ME (Book #1)
REACH ME (Book #2)
HIDE ME (Book #3)
BELIEVE ME (Book #4)
HELP ME (Book #5)
FORGET ME (Book #6)
HOLD ME (Book #7)
PROTECT ME (Book #8)
REMEMBER ME (Book #9)
CATCH ME (Book #10)
WATCH ME (Book #11)

RUBY HUNTER FBI SUSPENSE THRILLER
IF I RUN (Book #1)
IF I TELL (Book #2)
IF I LIVE (Book #3)

IF I FORGET (Book #4)
IF I RETURN (Book #5)

CAITLIN DARE FBI SUSPENSE THRILLER
COME GET ME (Book #1)
COME FIND ME (Book #2)
COME TAKE ME (Book #3)
COME CATCH ME (Book #4)
COME SAVE ME (Book #5)

REESE LINK MYSTERY
BEYOND REASON (Book #1)
BEYOND REACH (Book #2)
BEYOND REPAIR (Book #3)
BEYOND DOUBT (Book #4)
BEYOND NORMAL (Book #5)

Printed in Dunstable, United Kingdom

68569884R00092